THE BUNKER MURDERS

DI GILES BOOK 17

ANNA-MARIE MORGAN

ALSO BY ANNA-MARIE MORGAN

In the DI Giles Series:

Book 1 - Death Master

Book 2 - You Will Die

Book 3 - Total Wipeout

Book 4 - Deep Cut

Book 5 - The Pusher

Book 6 - Gone

Book 7 - Bone Dancer

Book 8 - Blood Lost

Book 9 - Angel of Death

Book 10 - Death in the Air

Book 11 - Death in the Mist

Book 12 - Death under Hypnosis

Book 13 - Fatal Turn

Book 14 - The Edinburgh Murders

Book 15 - A Picture of Murder

Book 16 - The Wilderness Murders

Book 17 - The Bunker Murders

Copyright © 2022 by Anna-marie Morgan

All rights reserved.

No part of this book may be reproduced in any form or by any electronic or mechanical means, including information storage and retrieval systems, without written permission from the author, except for the use of brief quotations in a book review.

For Jean and Christopher, with love

1

OLD BONES

"There's something here. I'm getting a helluva signal... I think it could be at least a foot long."

"A sword?"

Owen pulled a face. "I don't think a Roman sword would have survived in this soil. It is a powerful signal, though. Let's dig, see what we've got."

They set to work, shovelling the soil and tipping it to the side.

"What..." Fifty-four-year-old Tony stopped in his tracks. "There is something here... I think it's a skeleton."

"Has it got weapons?" His friend, twenty years his junior, peered at the bones sticking out of the dirt.

"I don't think this is a Roman find at all, Owen." Tony jabbed at a dirty rag with his spade. "I think this is a pair of jeans."

Owen stared at the muddy material, spotting a rusted metal stud. "That's not what gave us the signal, is it?"

"No, it was this..." The older man levered at the earth, exposing the item which had made their needle jump.

"Oh my God, it's a murder victim!" Owen cast his eyes

over the landscape, expecting a killer to spring from the mist hovering over the trees. He swallowed hard.

"Must be... I can't think of any other explanation."

"It's isolated up here. Maybe someone had a heart attack or died of exposure?"

"What? And buried themselves with a spade?" Tony grimaced.

"We'd better tell someone." Owen stared wide-eyed. "Stop digging. This could be a crime scene."

His friend scratched his head. "It has to be murder."

"I think we should leave."

"Agreed. I'm calling the police." Tony pulled out his mobile phone, swivelling it around with an outstretched arm. "Dammit no signal..."

Owen shuddered. "Let's get back to the truck. We can find a better spot. Take a photograph of the what we found, and you can send it to them."

∼

"Ma'am, phone call." Callum put his hand over the receiver. "It's Inspector Davies," he said, referring to the uniformed officer on the other end. "Line two."

"Thanks." She smoothed down her wool-mix skirt, taking the receiver. "DI Giles..." Her forehead creased in concentration. "We'll be right over."

"What's happened?" Dewi approached from his desk, hands in the pockets of his corduroys.

"They've found human remains in the fields above Garthowen housing estate."

"Murder victim?"

"It sounds like it. A couple of metal detectors looking for Roman artefacts found a shallow grave."

"Male or female?"

"Two guys, I think?" Yvonne raised a brow.

"I don't mean the prospectors." Dewi laughed. "I meant the remains."

"Oh..." She palmed her forehead. "They don't know until the pathologist has examined them. SOCO only just arrived. I thought we could head up there now, but grab your coat... It's raining."

Dewi followed her gaze to the window, and the darkening sky. "I'll drive."

"I won't argue with that." She collected her jacket and bag from the back of her chair. "Let's get up there before they remove the remains from the ground."

"Right you are."

2

JOHN DOE

The steep fields above Garthowen had been annexed by flashing lights, mechanical equipment, and people in plastic suits photographing, documenting and recovering the remains.

Drizzly rain had dampened the ground, and the mud sucked at their boots.

Yvonne approached a SOCO, kneeling next to the shallow grave. "Foul play?"

He pointed to his female colleague as she removed bones from the dirt, carefully cleaning some of the mud.

"Can't say for sure, but there is a sizeable nick in the sternum, and this left rib." She held it up. "Possibly damaged by a blade."

"Could the mark have been made with a shovel?" She asked, thinking of the prospectors who had discovered the remains.

She shook her head. "Unlikely... A shovel would have created more damage. It wouldn't have left such a clean cut."

"I see."

"We can't really tell you much until we have cleaned and examine these, you know that."

"Of course." Yvonne nodded. "When can we have the report?"

"We'll need a couple of days on this, at least. Hanson said he would have a look tomorrow morning," she said, referring to the pathologist.

"Fine." The DI cast her eyes along the field and hedge line. "It wouldn't be easy getting a body here," she said to Dewi. "Perhaps the victim was killed here?"

He nodded. "We are a significant distance from the main road. They may have been killed and hastily buried here. The covering soil was only a few inches deep."

"Except the shovel was buried with them." The female SOCO stood, temporarily straightening her knees as they clicked in complaint. "So whoever killed them either knew they were going to do so, or brought the spade along to bury a someone who was already deceased?"

Yvonne turned her gaze to where the land fell away toward the Severn Valley, and the nineteen-thirties housing estate peppered below. This was the sort of place one might come to contemplate the world, watch people from afar, admire a scenic Welsh landscape of rolling fields and big sky. It shouldn't be the place to find a murder victim.

She said so, taking a moment to contemplate this.

The heavens were angry, but the dark clouds somehow enriched the vibrant greenery below.

"The victim must have known the killer." She pursed her lips. "Perhaps they were lovers?"

Dewi grimaced. "Not a nice thought... Killed on a romantic walk."

"Well..." She sighed. "We needn't speculate until we have Hanson's report. Once we have the victim's sex and clothing description, we can run them through Missing Persons."

Dewi offered her a hand as they picked their way back down the hill to the main road, and where they had parked the car. The soft, greasy ground had them sliding as much as walking. A damp mist hovered over the trees.

~

Roger Hanson's postmortem report arrived three days later via email.

Yvonne pored over the details, tucking her cream blouse back into her charcoal pencil skirt.

Dewi placed a mug of tea in front of her. "What does he say?"

She leaned back in her chair, tapping her pen on her chin. "The victim was a middle-aged male in his early fifties, around five-foot-seven. He was wearing blue jeans, a red-check cotton shirt, and brown leather work boots when he died."

"That's a solid start..."

"Hanson thinks the victim was stabbed at least twice to the stomach and chest, the stab to the heart being the lethal wound. He can't give a definitive number of stabs, because he can only count the ones which hit bone, but the chest injury would have been enough to kill."

"Could have been a fight."

She nodded. "It was up close and personal, that's for sure. The victim had grey-brown hair. Putting everything together, we have a workable description to release to the public, and for searching MisPer. Could you ask Callum to look at it?"

"Will do." Dewi paused. "Are you going to do the press release?"

"I am. By the way, Hanson is having bone and soil samples analysed to give us a more accurate timeline. We'll know how long ago the body was buried. If we can tie it all in with a missing person, we'll be good to go."

She crossed the office to the interactive whiteboard, where photographs of the makeshift grave were displayed, and added the latest details for the victim. "What we need is your name," she said, gazing at the board, hands on hips. "Who were you?"

3

COLD AS THE GRAVE

"We have a match!" Callum announced, his dark hair dishevelled, a half-smoked cigarette tucked behind his ear, and a triumphant grin on his face.

Yvonne checked her watch. Less than an hour had passed since receiving Hanson's email. "Really?"

"I have one Malcolm Edwards of Plas Gwyn, Milford Road, in Newtown."

"Wow, that was quick."

He puffed his chest out. "No flies on me."

"Well..." She pointed to his notes. "Let's have the details?"

"If he is confirmed as our guy, he disappeared in two-thousand-and-five after popping off work for some lunch. The description of his clothing, his height and hair all match."

"And his age?"

"Fifty-three when he went missing."

"That sounds hopeful. Great work, Callum. Do we know if there's a DNA profile for him in the database?"

The Bunker Murders 9

"I'll chase it up and let you know." The DC closed his notebook. "I must admit, even I wasn't expecting to have the identity so soon. Being back on the nicotine is clearly having a beneficial effect, ma'am."

She grinned. "Any excuse not to give up... As for our victim, the hard work starts now."

"I know, I'm on it." He headed back to his desk.

At the afternoon briefing, Callum fleshed out their victim, the muscles in his face taut. "From everything I have gathered, Malcolm Edwards was a well-liked family man and a well-respected worker at Garvey-and-Griffiths Builder's Merchants, on the Mochdre Industrial Estate at the top of town. Nothing was too much trouble for him, and he was a favourite with staff and customers alike."

"So, not someone they would want to get rid of, then?" Yvonne rubbed her chin.

"Not according to the statements they gave."

"What about the day he disappeared? What do we know about his movements?"

Callum checked his notes. "He started work at eight-thirty that morning and, according to colleagues, was his usual self. It was a sunny June day, er... June sixth, to be exact. And as far as they could tell, the day was proceeding like any other. He told a colleague he was nipping out for lunch, which he did regularly, and didn't come back. His wife raised the alarm just after nine o'clock that night after ringing around friends and work colleagues. Police began the official search the following day."

The DI scratched her head. "Was his wife questioned about the disappearance? Had she any light to shed on where he might have gone during the lunchtime?"

"That was what got me thinking when I read the police report. When they talked to her, she was incoherent from the excessive use of prescribed valium, which she had taken on-and-off since her twenties to ease depression. The dosage was increased after Malcolm's disappearance. I think we should talk to her as soon as possible."

"Absolutely," Yvonne agreed. "Could you make a list of former colleagues, friends, and family members, and get them to me by tomorrow morning? We'll organise some interviews. Let's find out what we are dealing with, and why this man met with such a grisly end. No matter how nice Malcolm Edwards was, someone wanted him dead."

∼

THE DRIVE HOME took longer than usual that evening. Roadworks in the centre of town were followed by a slow-moving horse box, as urban thrum gave way to the verdant serenity of the countryside.

She tapped the steering wheel, her mind occupied by images of Malcolm Edwards in a muddy field above a housing estate. That they were his remains, had been confirmed by dental records. It was an ignominious end for an apparently popular man.

Dusk arrived when she did, February giving way to March. At least now, she could look forward to longer, warmer days. The winter would soon lose its bone-chilling grip on the world and Tasha would head home after working on another case in London.

Her head throbbing with a threatening migraine, she resolved to shower, eat, and have an early night. The following day, when questioning those who knew their cold case victim, she would have to be on her game.

4

THE GRIEVING WIDOW

Mrs Rhiannon Edwards still lived at Plas Gwyn, on the Milford Road, above Dolerw Park in Newtown. Thirteen years younger than her husband, she had been forty when he went missing.

Now in her late fifties, the former mid-wife stated on the phone she was retired, and concentrating on the regular baby-sitting of her grandchildren. She agreed to be alone in the house when the detectives called.

"Mrs Edwards?" Yvonne asked. "DI Giles, and DS Hughes."

"Yes, I'm Rhiannon Edwards." The woman, in a tee-shirt and lounge pants and with her grey hair cropped short, held open the door to her three-bedroomed detached home. "Come on through."

They followed her into a sizeable lounge with a view over the fields, trees, and the River Severn meandering through the park below.

The DI gazed at it, formulating the delicate words she would use to discuss that late Malcolm Edwards with the woman who had lost her lifelong companion.

"You've come about Mal." Rhiannon stated, looking directly at her.

Yvonne noted the widow's cool expression. "Yes, and we are very sorry for your loss. We-"

"I knew he was dead." The delivery was matter-of-fact. Deadpan.

The DI cleared her throat. "We are putting together a timeline for his movements leading up to his disappearance and murder in June two-thousand-five."

Mrs Edwards turned to the window.

"We believe he was murdered by someone he knew."

She returned her gaze to them and shrugged. "What do you want to know?"

Yvonne raised a brow.

"It's been seventeen years, Inspector. It's not so raw anymore. I can talk about him without breaking down. I'm sorry if that surprises you."

"It's okay... I understand." She did, but Mrs Edwards' cool demeanour had her wondering. "Can you remember how he was in himself, in the days leading up to his disappearance?"

"As far as I can remember, he was fine. He ate his breakfast with me at eight that morning and was looking forward to his day."

"Did he ever meet you for lunch on a workday?"

Rhiannon shook her head.

"Did he ever come home to see you during his workday?"

"No."

"Where-"

"Tell a lie," Mrs Edwards interjected. "He came home during a workday the once. It was in the week prior to my sister's wedding. He had to try on his suit for the tailor.

Otherwise, he never did. He sometimes used lunch breaks to visit customer projects, though, especially if it helped further sales. He was a very popular store assistant. Shoppers gravitated toward him because he really knew his stuff. Mal was good at technical things, and a natural problem-solver. My husband was a friend to many of his customers, not just a sales assistant, and he had a kind face."

"Did he mention the need to go anywhere else on the day he disappeared? Do you know if he had a lunchtime appointment with a customer that day?" Yvonne cocked her head, scrutinising Rhiannon's face.

Mrs Edwards shrugged. "I only know that he left work that lunchtime. He sometimes went to a local snack shop on the estate, or he would walk up the lane with his sandwiches. He liked the views up there."

"But you don't know if he did any of those things on that day?"

"He may have." Rhiannon sighed. "He simply didn't mention it. Mal wasn't in the habit of telling me his plans. If he was in the mood, and he had the time and the inclination, he would just take a wander."

"I see."

"He used to say that planning too much took away the fun."

"He liked spontaneity?"

"Yes, he did."

"Were you working at the time?"

"I was a Newtown mid-wife, working a reduced caseload. After my children were born, I returned to work part time. I went full time again after they had grown up, but I retired when the Covid pandemic struck."

"And your children were still very young when your husband disappeared?"

"Yes... Sonya, our oldest, was twelve. Tom was ten. They were devastated when their dad didn't come home."

"I'll bet." Yvonne pressed her lips together, her gaze softened by empathy. "What about you? What were your thoughts?"

"I feared the worst right from the beginning. It wasn't like Mal to not come home. He wouldn't have done that. He would never abandon his family. I knew in my heart something bad had happened. I felt it..."

"You told police you knew of no-one who would want to hurt your husband. Did that change at all? Were you aware of his disagreeing with anyone? Did you or any of his friends have suspicions?"

Rhiannon shook her head.

"Did Mal keep a diary or a notepad?"

"He kept a diary... He didn't write in it every day. It was more of an aide-mémoire, really, so he wouldn't forget something important."

"I see. Do you still have it?"

She nodded. "It's in a drawer upstairs."

"May we have it for a while?"

"Of course, I'll get it for you." Mrs Edwards headed for the living room door. "I'll be back in a minute."

"Thank you." Yvonne closed her notebook.

When Rhiannon returned, she held a dark-brown leather notebook in her hand, briefly thumbing through the pages before handing it over.

Yvonne noted the scuffed exterior and dog-eared pages. Someone had spent long hours poring over its contents.

The meniscus of tears in Mrs Edwards' eyes left the DI in no doubt who the likely person was. "Thank you. We will return Mal's book as soon as we have finished with it."

The woman nodded, blowing her nose into her hanky. "Please."

"We will keep you fully informed of our progress."

"Thank you."

"But, should you have any further thoughts regarding the motive for your husband's murder or if you hear anything you think is relevant, contact us... Contact us right away."

"I will let you know."

Yvonne and Dewi walked back to the car in silence, lost in their thoughts of Mal, and what happened to him. How, and why, had such an amiable man met such a horrible death?

The DI hoped his colleagues could shed some light.

5

ABDUCTION

"M a'am?" DC Dai Clayton grabbed her as soon as she walked in.

"Yes?" She threw her padded jacket over the back of her chair.

"The DCI wants us on a missing person case, says it requires urgent attention."

"Okay... What are we looking at?" She checked her watch, her stomach rumbling.

Dai ran a hand through his newly clipped, dark hair while scratching his forehead with the opposite thumbnail. "Nineteen-year-old female, Kate Hughes, disappeared while riding her bike home from Newtown College, where she is studying art. The bike was found in the canal, but there was no sign of the girl."

"How long has she been missing?" she asked, eyes drawn to the perfect knot in Clayton's tie.

"She disappeared sometime between three-fifteen and four o'clock. I am told we have CCTV for some of her journey along the river and canal towpaths, but nothing for the journey out at Llanllwchaiarn. There were no cameras working out that far."

"Have they recovered the bike from the canal?"

"They have, ma'am."

"Fingerprints?"

"I understand they have taken it for testing. No results have come back yet."

"Okay thanks, Dai. Can you give me everything you have and get a hold of all relevant footage for the Kate's journey? If she cycled every day along the same route, it would be good to have CCTV for the days leading up to her disappearance, if we can get it. If she was abducted, whoever took her may have been stalking her prior."

"I suspect an abduction, because the bike ended up in the canal and, if she had fallen in and drowned, her body would have been found by now. Her parents are insisting she wouldn't disappear voluntarily. They said she doesn't have a boyfriend."

"Make sure of that, will you, Dai?" Yvonne rubbed her chin. "Find out who her closest friends are, and if there are any current or former partners - anyone who may have had a motive to take her."

"Will do, ma'am."

"Young women do not tell their parents everything, even if they are still living at home."

"Thought you might need this." Dewi plopped a steaming mug down on her desk. "I know I did."

"You read my mind, Dewi. Thank you." She grimaced. "We'll need plenty of caffeine with two big cases on the go."

"Why what's happened?" He frowned.

The DI filled him in.

"Next week is out then?" he asked, referring to her planned leave.

She shrugged. "Perhaps it's just as well. Tasha is away on another case in London, and I hadn't planned to go anywhere. I'll cancel the leave and get on with it."

"Everyone needs a break, Yvonne." Dewi studied her face. "Don't overdo it."

"I hear you, Dewi." She nodded. "In the meantime, can you get on to Garvey-and-Griffiths Builder's Merchants, and set up a meeting for us with the manager and any staff remaining from the time Mal Edwards worked there?"

"Will do... What are you planning?"

"I'm going back up to the gravesite. I have a hunch Mal left work that day to wander up the lane with his sandwiches. Perhaps someone accompanied him, or forced him to accompany them, and made him walk further than he intended, given that he would have been late back to work. I want to have a gander in the area, so I can make sense of it."

"Right you are."

~

Yvonne could see why Mal Edwards had enjoyed taking his sandwiches up the lane at the back of the Mochdre Industrial Estate.

She took the route she thought most likely for his stroll, walking only fifteen minutes as his breaks were usually only thirty minutes to an hour long.

There were more factories peppering the view than there would have been in Mal's time, but the nestled town and hills beyond would have provided a similarly perfect view for a man taking time out from his busy schedule advising DIY customers on how to use various tools, or the best kit for their project.

There was a glaring problem with the walk theory,

however. She was still some distance from the spot where Mal's remains were found and where, they believed, he had been murdered. Even with wellingtons to protect from the brambles, the onward amble through the fields, over connecting stiles, took at least another twenty minutes. Mal would have no reason, and not enough time, to go that far to each his lunch. His break would have been eaten up by the time to get there.

No, she was convinced that he wouldn't have walked that far if he had intended going back to work that afternoon. Either he had no intention of returning, or someone had met him on his break and lured or forced him into going with them. That person was probably fully aware of his or her victim's routine.

6

KATE

Kate and her parents, Della and Tom Hughes, inhabited a three-bedroomed detached home off the Upper Canal Road, near to Newtown hospital.

The drive to their house was steep and winding. Still in her wellingtons, Yvonne thought she had better retrieve her shoes from the boot before approaching their front door. It wouldn't do to leave a mess on the welcome mat.

Forty-five-year-old Della opened the door.

The DI noted the smudged mascara below the mother's eyes and the deep worry-lines on her forehead. She suspected Mrs Hughes had slept little since her daughter's disappearance.

"Mrs Hughes?" Yvonne tilted her head. "DI Giles..."

"Yes..." Della took a step backward, allowing the DI over the threshold, into the tiny hallway.

"I wanted to talk with you about your daughter."

"Do you have news?" Mrs Hughes's eyes widened.

"I'm afraid not." The DI's gaze was soft. "I would like a

better understanding of Kate and what has been going on in her life."

Della nodded. "Of course... I'm afraid my husband, Tom, is out at work."

"That's okay. I'm sure you can tell me what I need to know."

"I'll do what I can. Ask away."

"Thank you." Yvonne followed the tiny-framed woman through to a south-facing lounge, warmed by the sun, and occupied by a sizeable suite of furniture that included a corner piece sofa with a grey-velvet finish.

Two empty cups occupied a polished mahogany coffee table along with a photo of a smiling teenage Kate standing between her mum and dad, the sun setting over the sea.

Della moved cushions around on the sofa for the DI to sit.

"Mrs Hughes-"

"It's Della."

"Della... Does Kate always cycle home after college?"

"Yes, unless the weather is bad, she always cycles. My daughter worries about the environment and insists on doing her bit."

"What time were you expecting her home yesterday?"

Mrs Hughes scratched her head, her gaze on the window. "She usually gets in between quarter-to-four and four o'clock, depending on the traffic and weather."

"Does she ever stay late?"

"She sometimes has an evening lecture, or meets her friends after college."

"Had she planned anything like that yesterday?"

Della shook her head. "She told me before she left in the morning that she would be home by four."

"And she always sticks to her plans?"

"Yes, or she warns me if there has been a change and she is going to be delayed. Kate always tells us where she'll be. She knows we worry otherwise."

"I see... Did you hear from her at all during the day yesterday?" The DI scribbled in her notebook.

"No, I didn't. She sometimes texts, but not every day. Often, it's asking me what I'm making for dinner. She would have texted if she had intended coming home late."

"And there was nothing else to show a change in her itinerary? As you know, we found her bike. Could Kate have had an accident and gone to a friend's house? Somewhere without a phone signal? Do any of her friends live in areas with poor coverage?"

"No, she would have phoned me if something had happened... Or asked her friends to. She would not have left us hanging."

"Does your daughter have a best friend?"

"That would be Debbie Taylor. She and Kate are close."

"Have you spoken with Debbie?"

"We contacted her about seven o'clock last night. She said she hadn't seen Kate since they left college shortly after three."

"I see... May I?" Yvonne picked up the photo from the coffee table.

"Sure." Della nodded. "I picked that out for you. We gave officers another one yesterday, but the one you are holding is more recent. It was taken last week. Tom had it printed at the chemist's last night."

Yvonne took in the long blonde hair and wide smile. "She's a lovely girl, Della."

"She is." Mrs Hughes nodded, her brow furrowed. "I'm scared..."

"You know we can request access to her social media

accounts? My team is working on them at the moment. We can access photographs and contacts, and examine any connections that may be suspect."

"Suspect?"

"If your daughter was abducted, she may have been stalked beforehand."

"Oh, God... She's on Facebook and TikTok. That's it, I think?"

"We should be able to access her profiles." The DI rubbed her chin. "Has your daughter ever mentioned receiving unwanted attention? Was she followed home, for instance?"

Della pursed her lips. "Not for a while... There was a young man a few months back. Stuart, his name was. Stuart Benham. He asked her out on a date two or three times, and she turned him down. I asked Kate why she said no, and she said he wasn't her type. She thought he was too immature for her."

"I see... Do I take it he didn't try again after that?"

"I can't say for sure, but she hasn't mentioned him for at least two months, so I assumed he gave up. Perhaps, he didn't?"

"Is he a fellow college student?"

Mrs Hughes nodded.

Yvonne made notes. "Same course?"

"I think so..."

"Well, we'll certainly look into Mr Benham, and speak to Kate's friend Debbie. In the meantime, if you hear anything else, or if Kate gets touch, please let us know straightaway."

"I will."

"And, just to be clear, Kate hasn't run away before or stayed away unexpectedly?"

"Never." Mrs Hughes' gaze was steadfast. "This is completely out of character."

"Understood." The DI gave her a reassuring smile as she rose from her seat. "We'll do everything we can to get your daughter back to you."

Della nodded. "Thank you, DI Giles."

∽

"Any news on Kate Hughes, Dai?" she asked, on returning to the office.

"We got hold of the existing footage of Kate's journey home. We should have the rest by the end of the play today. Callum said he was happy to stay late this evening to go through it. I am making a start this afternoon."

"That's great... My plan is to go with Dewi to see the manager at Garvey-and-Griffiths, and find out what they remember of Mal."

"Before you go, I should tell you that witnesses living along the towpath said they saw a scruffy white van parked alongside the canal at Llanllwchaiarn yesterday afternoon. It was also there for a couple of hours the day before. They are adamant they hadn't seen it there before. The house owner closest said they will keep an eye out for it this afternoon, in case it returns. They didn't get a registration, but they will if it comes back. I'm hoping we can get it from the CCTV footage if we've caught it on camera."

"Great." Yvonne nodded. "What about fingerprints on Kate's bike? Did they find any?"

Dai shook his head. "They didn't even find Kate's. So, either she wiped it clean before tossing it in the canal, or her abductor did. If a perpetrator wiped it down, they likely were not wearing gloves when they snatched her. This could be an opportunistic crime."

"I'm fearing the worst, Dai. After speaking with her mum, I do not believe Kate would wish her parents to worry. I think something untoward happened yesterday, so please go through everything with a fine-tooth comb."

"Will do."

7

DEAD MAN'S WORK

The Garvey-and-Griffiths Builder's Merchants was a massive store, populated by aisle after aisle of hardware and materials, floor to ceiling.

Yvonne mused the sheer range of goods would feel overwhelming to her if she needed something. She could understand how a helpful assistant like Mal Edwards would make a significant difference to customer's purchase decisions, especially if, like her, they didn't know where to start.

"Can I help you?" A bespectacled man in his mid-thirties with tussled, mousy hair approached them, likely because of the lost look on the DI's face.

"Yes, thank you. We're looking for Don Akeman or Simon Jones?" She referred to the men who had worked there since Mal's time.

"Ah, yes..." He nodded, pushing his glasses up his nose. "Don Akeman is the manager. I think Simon may be at lunch. I'll go see if Don is out the back."

"Thanks," Dewi answered, hands deep in his pockets. He turned to the DI. "I can see why staff might want to get out for a bit at lunchtime. I'm worn out just looking at all this."

Yvonne grinned. "You're certainly spoiled for choice..."

"DI Giles?"

She swung round to the origin of the gravelly voice, raising her brows.

"Don Akeman." The stocky older man with peppery-grey hair wiped a hand on the front of his overalls before extending it.

"Mr Akeman." She shook the offered hand. It was firm and dry. "I'm here to talk to you about Malcolm Edwards, your former colleague-"

"Ah yes, Mal." He cleared his throat, looking at the marbled-vinyl floor tiles. "I heard the news... We often wondered what happened to him. It's awful that he ended up in that muddy field. It couldn't have happened to a nicer guy." He sighed. "Would you like to come through to the office? Dave can look after the customers."

She guessed Dave must be the young man with glasses who had greeted them on arrival. "Yes, that would be good."

"Come in," he instructed, closing the door behind them as they stepped into a room close to chaos, with piles of paper, invoice books, and manuals sporting stains from the bottoms of coffee cups. "Excuse the mess in here." He pulled out two wooden chairs for them, as a printer in the corner spewed several pages. "Can I get you a cuppa?"

The DI eyed the dusty kettle on a table at the back.

Both officers shook their heads.

"Do you mind if I have one?"

"Not at all..." Yvonne checked her watch. It was almost two o'clock.

"How can I help?" he asked, returning with a mug and two digestives.

"We believe you knew Mal well?"

"I knew him reasonably well, yes. I worked with him for about three years until he vanished. He seemed a thoroughly decent bloke, and one of the most helpful men I knew. He was twenty years my senior. I respected him as a mentor. He had a wealth of experience, I remember that."

"Did he eat alone?"

"He often had his lunch in here, usually with whoever else was on lunch at the same time. Occasionally, he went out with his sandwiches for a walk up the lane, or wandered around the industrial estate. It's sometimes nice to have a change of scenery. Occasionally he popped out to see a customer's work-in-progress, if they needed practical advice."

"And the day he disappeared, did he go out with his lunch?"

He screwed his face up. "I believe so... It was a long time ago now, mind. But I seem to remember that he took his lunch, yes."

"And he never returned."

"He didn't come back. He was absent all afternoon, and it was the talk of the store. It wasn't like Mal to vanish without telling somebody. Several customers asked about him as he had agreed to help them that day, so we knew the disappearance was planned. We didn't know until the following day that he was missing. His wife phoned us in the morning in tears."

"Did he ever discuss his personal life with you? Or anything else?"

Don shrugged. "Well, there was a bit of an age difference between us... We were into different things, really. I mean, we'd discuss our weekends and such and who had won the football, but I can't remember discussing anything more personal with him."

"Nothing about his relationship?"

"Not that I can recall. Nothing that jumps out at me. But then, like I say, it was a long time ago. I sometimes struggle to remember conversations I had yesterday, let alone seventeen years ago." He took a long sip from his mug of tea.

"Did you hear any rumours about his disappearance? Did you have any suspicions regarding what had happened to him? What were people saying?"

He shook his head. "I don't think he was one to have an affair, and I didn't hear of any if there was one. I always saw Mal as a private person, one who kept work and home life separate. He was outgoing with the customers, but kept his personal life quiet."

"I see." Yvonne cast Dewi a glance. "I understand there is another member of staff here who also knew Mal?"

"Yes, that would be Simon Jones. He should be back in the shop by now."

She nodded. "We'd like to speak to him, if that is possible?"

Akeman lost part of his biscuit in his tea. He stared at the liquid, frowning in disappointment. "I don't know if he would know any more than I do-"

"We would still like to chat to him." The DI fixed him with a level gaze, clear blue eyes giving nothing away.

"Right..." He cleared his throat, rising from the table. "I'll go get him."

∼

AT SIX-FOOT-THREE, Simon Jones filled the door frame.

Yvonne stood as he entered the room, which seemed almost too small for him.

He perched on another of the wooden chairs, his thigh protruding over the sides. "How can I help?" he asked, tilting his head, making them feel he was really listening.

She imagined him developing that skill over many years dealing with customers. "We're here to talk to you about Mal Edwards. Are you aware his remains were found last week in a field above Garthowen?" Yvonne leaned towards him. "I understand he was your friend?"

Jones nodded, his stare going through and beyond her. "I would say we were quite good friends. He was always there for me, and took me under his wing when I first started here at Garvey-and-Griffiths."

"I understand you were a teenager at the time?"

"I turned twenty in my first year here. Mal went missing when I was twenty-five. I'd known him for five years, and got to understand him well during that time. He had a good heart and was brilliant with the customers."

"Yes, we'd heard that he was popular with shoppers who needed advice."

"Oh, definitely... He would visit their projects if they asked him to, and advise on equipment and tools that would help them. He went above and beyond, and I don't think he was rewarded enough for that."

"Are you saying you think he should have earned more?"

"Mal would never have said that. He was happy to get the bonus at Christmas. He was a genuine guy who enjoyed helping people. With or without the extra money, he would have done the same thing. He treated many returning customers like friends, and Newtown was a lot like that back then. It's a small town. Everyone knew each other's business even before social media."

The DI nodded. "Did you ever come across anyone who was not friendly with Mal? Did you see him disagreeing with anyone?"

Jones shook his head. "Not really, no... I never saw him have an argument. He was one of those people with endless patience, even with the most difficult of customers."

"He sounds like a saint." She scoured his face.

He frowned. "The fact Mal was polite and helpful out there didn't mean he was always happy. I saw him with his head in his hands a few times. Things got to him, but he could usually pick himself up afterwards." He rubbed his forehead with the back of his hand and rolled up the sleeves on his red cotton shirt. "I've lost my temper a few times with awkward customers, but I never saw Mal do that. If he became annoyed, he internalised it."

"I see. Did you socialise with him out of work?"

"We had the occasional work do, like Christmas parties, but Mal was a family man foremost. He never came on a pub crawl with us, preferring to stay in and watch telly with his wife. Occasionally, he would put the odd bet on football, or the horses, but nothing too big or too often. He was just a regular guy with a big heart."

"Did you ever go out for lunch with him?"

"No."

"Where were you on the day he disappeared?"

"I was right here... All day." He leaned back in the chair, holding her gaze. "I noticed he wasn't around much that afternoon, but I got on with things. It wasn't until the next day that I realised he was missing. It was quite a shock, I can tell you."

"I'll bet it was..." She rubbed her chin.

"Listen, I'd better get back out there. Dave is on the shop floor on his own." Jones rose from his seat.

Yvonne also stood. "Here's my card... If you think of anything else we ought to know, please call. It doesn't matter how significant you think it is."

He accepted the card. "I will."

8

THE MEN ON THE WALL

Callum and Dai had been poring over CCTV footage all morning, with ties loosened, hand-combed hair unkempt, and Callum smoking very few cigarettes, leaving him ragged and desperate for a fix.

"Been busy, boys?" Yvonne grinned at seeing the state of them.

Callum pulled a face. "Did you bring sandwiches?"

"No..." Dewi plopped a white cardboard box down on the desk. "But we brought cakes from Evans's," he stated, referring to the popular cafe in town that made amazing cakes.

"Bargain!" Dai threw open the lid, eyes brighter than they had been for a while.

"I'll put the kettle on." Yvonne left her coat and bag in a heap.

Rejuvenated by the sugar and caffeine, the DC duo outlined their findings from the footage.

"We have the images from five street cameras and three buildings," Dai began. "The establishments include the Cambrian pub on the corner of Cambrian Street. They've enabled us to tie in the footage from the towpath with local comings and goings during the middle part of Kate Hughes' Bike journey."

"Okay, great." Yvonne took a sip of tea to wash down a mouthful of Chelsea bun.

"We see Kate pass on her bicycle in the frames beginning at three-seventeen. From then until three-twenty, she is watched by these characters." Dai zoomed in on his laptop to two figures sitting atop the town wall bordering the carpark. "These two were on the wall opposite the Cambrian and the Newtown Kebab House."

"Who are they?" Dewi asked, peering at the screen.

Callum answered. "I contacted the kebab place, and we believe they are Reza Hassani and Ahmed Syeed. They are young Iraqi men appealing asylum applications which were turned down. They hang around the area a lot apparently and have friends who work at the kebab shop and the barber's next door to it. We think it's curious that these two watched Kate for several minutes. Even if they are not connected to her disappearance, they may have seen something."

The DI rubbed her chin. "They seem to watch her intently."

"They do and, although it may be innocent, I think we should talk to them. See what they have to say."

"Agreed." Yvonne nodded. "Can you set up interviews with them both?"

"Will do." Dai nodded.

"Sorry guv," Callum grimaced. "I'm dying for a fag."

Yvonne threw her head back in mock exasperation. "Go on, choke your airways, but you know you'll regret it," she said, referring to his umpteen unsuccessful attempts to give up.

Callum waved, already half-way through the door.

∼

THE DI TOOK advantage of a quieter period to examine the small leather notebook that had belonged to Mal Edwards.

He hadn't written in it every day. There were regular gaps in the entries, sometimes for several days. It seemed to comprise notes on the good and bad points of equipment supplied by the shop, as relayed to him by customer experience, and the details of meetings with suppliers and project managers.

Although not himself a manager at Garvey-and-Griffiths, the actual manager had trusted Mal to liaise with manufacturers and clients alike. Edwards appeared to have relished the responsibility. Many of the entries were in pencil, with only the occasional use of ink.

She flipped to the weeks immediately preceding Mal's disappearance, scouring each entry for reasons he might have left the warehouse on the day he vanished.

Dewi joined her. "Anything jump out at you?"

"Not yet." She sighed. "He regularly met with people outside of the store, including suppliers and customers. There is nothing to show a particular problem or disagreement. If difficulties arose in his last weeks, he didn't mention them. There's just a list of appointments, notes, and sketches of customer projects."

Her sergeant nodded. "We could speak to his children?"

"We could, but I doubt they would remember much. Sonya and Tom were twelve and ten. I don't think they'll have much to add." Her gaze travelled back to the book. "I have a feeling the answer may be somewhere in here, though. I think I'll take it home with me... My bedtime reading for a while."

"Tasha is still away, then?" Dewi inclined his head, searching her face.

"She's working a tough case for the Met. I don't think she'll be back for at least another week."

"We should have the report back from forensics on Mal's remains tomorrow. They found fibres on his jeans. We're unlikely to match them with anything. It's been so long, but who knows? Perhaps the killer still has a jumper or coat in the back of their wardrobe that they wore seventeen years ago?"

Yvonne grimaced. "Dewi, I love your optimism."

Callum joined her at her desk, the faint whiff of smoke emanating from his jacket. "Ma'am, we've examined the CCTV footage for several of the days prior to Kate Hughes's disappearance."

"Okay..."

"On two out of the three days we looked at, Hassani and Syeed were seated on that wall, watching the river path, at the time Kate passes through."

"Is Kate in the footage?"

Callum nodded. "We think she was captured by cameras on all three days."

"What do you mean, *think*?"

"We are going on her outfit, helmet, and general shape, as we can't really see her face very well under the helmet."

"And the two Iraqis were watching her?"

"Yes." Callum placed his hands on his hips.

"What about the other passers-by? Were the two men also watching them?"

"They were, but we think they paid particular attention to Kate."

"Right-"

"There's something else."

"Go on…"

"On the day she vanished, a couple of minutes after Kate cycled by them, Ahmed and Reza disappeared from the wall."

"Really?" She frowned. "Did they jump down? Do we have it on tape?"

"We see them getting down on the opposite side of the wall to Kate, and they head off on foot along the river path towards McDonald's. They may have accessed the canal towpath after that. Unfortunately, the store's CCTV doesn't stretch to the area they would have entered the towpath. So we do not know if they used that route."

"Good work, Callum. I would like to interview both of them as soon as possible. Also, can you check whether either of them has criminal records?"

"Will do."

"In the meantime, there is a male friend of Kate's I would like to speak to speak to. I'm meeting him at the college this afternoon. So, the earliest I can see Ahmed or Reza would be four o'clock this afternoon."

"No problem, I'll get them in today if possible. Failing that, tomorrow."

9

YOUNG MAN SCORNED

Stuart Benham waited for her by Coleg Powys's reception double-door, biting his lip, and pacing. In a khaki jacket and trainers, with a canvas bag over hunched shoulders, hands pushed deep in his jeans pockets, he looked up to no good. She wondered if he realised this.

He approached, head cocked.

She judged him to be around five-feet-eleven. "Stuart?" she asked, as he came close.

He nodded, looking around. "Is it okay to go somewhere? I'd rather not talk here."

"Sure." Yvonne narrowed her eyes. "My car is just around the corner. We can sit in that, if you like? We should get out of the wind."

"Great." He ran a hand through longish blonde hair, casting a glance behind.

"You look nervous." Her eyes searched his face as he settled into her vehicle. "What are you afraid of?"

"I'm not afraid..." His forehead creased. "I don't want my friends to see me talking to police."

"Why?" It was her turn to frown.

"Well, with Kate missing, everyone is looking for someone to blame."

"And you think they'll suspect you of doing something to her?"

"They might if they see me talking to you."

"I could be anyone, surely?"

He shrugged. "The rumour mill grinds like crazy around here. Speculation is rampant on social media. People are being hung out to dry."

Yvonne nodded. "We'll be looking at that. I understand you dated Kate for a while? And that you split up a couple of months ago?"

"See?" He sighed. "I knew it."

"What do you mean, Stuart? Are you saying you didn't see each other?"

"We did... But it was hardly boyfriend-girlfriend stuff. Don't get me wrong," he added, running his tongue over his bottom lip. "I find her attractive, and would have liked to have seen more of her, but she is non-committal, really. We had coffee together, and I took her for a curry twice in town. But, other than that, we were not involved."

"Did you ask her for more?"

"I tried to kiss her one night after taking her for a meal. I'd had a few drinks."

"How did she respond?"

He turned to gaze through the window opposite, biting his lower lip. "She pushed me away."

"How did you react?"

"I accepted she didn't want the contact and backed off. I'm not saying I wasn't disappointed..."

When he turned back to her, the DI noted the beads of

sweat on his brow. "Where were you when you attempted the kiss?" She had CCTV in mind.

"We were on the grounds of Dolerw Park. We'd taken a stroll by the river."

"What happened after that?"

"I walked her back into the town centre, watched her get into a taxi, and walked home through the park to my parent's house in Vaynor. I remember feeling disappointed and low, but I'm a big boy. At least we would be friends, and I respected her decision. To be described as her ex-boyfriend is taking things too far. We simply had a few friendly dates."

"I see. Did you go on any other casual dates with her after that?"

"We had coffee once or twice during the day at college. That's about it. I didn't really feel comfortable asking her out after the night of the kiss."

"What about other male friends?"

"What do you mean?"

"Did anyone else ask her out after you did? Did she talk to any other guys?"

He shook his head. "She was focussed on art projects for her course. I don't think she dated anyone else. I wasn't aware of others, anyway." He shrugged.

Yvonne checked her watch. "Well, thank you for taking the time out of your day to speak with me."

"I wish I could have been more help." He scratched his head, eyes back on the window.

"We're hoping she will still turn up but, if you hear anything we ought to know, Stuart, call us." She handed him a card from her bag. "It doesn't matter how trivial you think the information."

"Yes, okay." He put the card in his jacket pocket. Some of the colour had returned to his face.

~

"Ahmed Syeed is waiting in interview room one," Callum announced on her return. "He is with an interpreter."

"Great." She whipped her jacket off. "What about Reza Hassani?"

"Scheduled for first thing tomorrow morning." The DC pulled a face. "The interpreter, Salim Abadeh, cannot be with us more than an hour, as he is travelling up to Wrexham later. He said he can be back for tomorrow's session with Reza."

She nodded. "Okay, that will have to do. Thanks, Callum."

"No worries."

~

Though Ahmed Syeed and Salim Abadeh hailed from the same country, they inhabited vastly distinct realities.

Salim wore a business suit and tie, his short hair in a stylish angular cut. He spoke with confidence, and the air of someone with a busy diary.

Ahmed Syeed was ten years younger than his interpreter, according to his stated age of twenty-two, and attended in jeans, tee-shirt, and scuffed muddy trainers. He sported a small goatee, and his tousled curly hair needed a trim.

Syeed slumped in the chair, a scowl on his drawn face. He exchanged words with the interpreter as she organised her papers.

Yvonne raised a brow, looking at Abadeh.

"He asks if this will take long? He says he has offered to help his friend at the kebab shop later," the interpreter advised.

"Well, that will depend on Ahmed, but we hope not to keep either of you any more than an hour." She pulled her seat closer to the desk, waiting for Abadeh to relay this information. "Ahmed, I understand you spend a lot of time in and around Newtown Kebab House?"

"Yes," he confirmed via Abadeh.

"You regularly sit on the wall opposite the shop?"

"Yes." Ahmed shifted in his seat, his hands under the table.

"You enjoy watching the world go by?"

Ahmed shrugged. "I talk with my friend."

The DI raised both brows. "You speak English?"

"I have a bit of English, yes."

She nodded. "Your friend... Is that Reza Hassani?"

"Yes."

"I understand you are both from Iraq?"

"We escaped the war. Was really bad." He shook his head. "Long time now we wait for asylum. They say have no case. Can go back now to Iraq. But not safe for us."

"I see..." She slid two photographs towards Syeed. They were of Kate. One showed her in cycling gear, the other was in her normal clothing, and with her face and hair exposed. "Ahmed, do you recognise this girl?"

His eyes lingered on Kate's face. "No." He rubbed his forehead.

"Are you sure?"

"Yes." He grunted to clear his throat.

"You don't recognise her?"

"Why should I?"

"This woman is missing. She disappeared while cycling home along the river and canal on the way to Llanllwchaiarn."

He shrugged, exchanging words with the interpreter.

"Ahmed would like to know what the missing girl has to do with him?"

She pushed another photograph forward. This time, it was a still image from the CCTV showing Syeed and Hassani sitting on the wall, watching Kate in her cycle gear. "Does this ring any bells?"

Ahmed shook his head, licking his upper lip.

"Please take a really good look."

He picked up the image, studying it for several seconds. "I don't know... Maybe..."

"Is that you in the photograph?"

He sighed. "Yes."

"And your friend Reza?"

"Yes, we sitting on wall talking."

"Okay... The girl in that image is Kate. She was on her way home."

He again swapped words with his interpreter.

"Ahmed says he doesn't remember seeing her."

Yvonne pushed forward another image. It showed both Ahmed and his friend in different clothing, watching Kate on the towpath. "This was taken the day after the one I just showed you."

Syeed paled. "What is this, please? I know nothing about this girl."

"Really? You don't remember seeing her? Watching her?"

A rapid-fire exchange took place between Ahmed and his interpreter.

"He insists he doesn't recognise the woman."

"How well does he know his friend, Reza Hassani?" She waited while they discussed it.

"He says he has known him for a long time. They stay in the same house. They met at a refugee centre," Abadeh informed her.

"I see... Does anyone else live in the house? Who is your landlord?"

"He tells me his landlord is a taxi driver in town and also lives at the house with Ahmed and Reza."

"And this house is on Commercial Street, in Newtown?"

"Yes." This time, Ahmed answered for himself.

"How long have you lived there?"

"Since three months."

"And how long has Reza lived there?"

"Same."

The DI narrowed her eyes. "Are you sure you don't remember this young woman?"

"Am sure."

Yvonne pressed her lips together, knowing she couldn't continue without proof they had interacted with Kate. "Very well, we're done here. Thank you for coming in."

∽

"Any joy?" Dewi caught up with her in the corridor.

She shook her head, rolling the sleeves of her blouse up. "He claims not to remember seeing Kate at all."

"Do you believe him?"

She pursed her lips. "I really don't know. One thing I am sure of, however. His English is a lot better than I expected. Something tells me he may not have needed the interpreter at all."

Dewi nodded. "You might be right. I rang the kebab

house and spoke to the owner. He said both Ahmed and Reza are capable of conversational English."

"Right well, we'll see what Reza has to say for himself. I'm considering a friendly visit to their house later tomorrow. Speak to the landlord."

"Sure." The DS rubbed the back of his neck. "Don't forget you have an appointment with Kate's friend, Debbie Taylor. She's coming in at three this afternoon."

"Thank you, Dewi." She checked her watch. "Where does the time go?"

∼

"Ah, Yvonne... Come in." DCI Llewelyn put his phone down, pushing the chair back from his desk. "How are things going?" His mussed hair and loose tie suggested a fraught afternoon.

"Progress is slower than I would have liked." She grimaced. "We've had no news on Kate Hughes, and we don't yet have a motive for the murder of Malcolm Edwards, our cold case."

"Oh, dear..."

"We are working through his friends and family, however, and the community is helping to spread the word about Kate."

"Do you think she wanted to disappear?" he rose from his chair to grab the coffeepot from the percolator at the back of his office. "Want one?"

"No, thank you." She shook her head. "Honestly? I can't prove she didn't choose to go somewhere, but I doubt it. I am convinced after talking to her mother, her disappearance is out of character. That, added to the fact we found her bike in the canal, makes me think something untoward happened. It was a fairly new bike. She had only had it for six months. And it was expensive."

"I see..." Llewelyn nodded. "I trust your intuition. How are things at home?" He met her gaze.

"Okay, quiet... Tasha is away and, to be honest, I'm glad I have two cases on the go."

"Will she be gone long?"

"I don't know, it depends on the work. She called me last night. She said she's guiding their suspect interviews, and it could be another week before she can get some time at home."

"I'm sorry." Llewelyn cocked his head. "Well, don't overdo it, Yvonne. Everyone needs downtime, even when they don't know what to do with it because their partner is away." He winked at her.

She grinned. "I'll bear that in mind, but I'd better get back to it, sir. I've got Kate Hughes's best friend coming in less than five minutes."

"Right, off you go." He nodded. "Thanks for the updates."

10

BEST FRIENDS?

Everything about Kate Hughes' best friend Debbie was long. Fingernails, frame, and dark hair. She was at least eighteen inches taller than Yvonne, and casually smart in a pink blouse and jeans.

"Thank you for coming in." The DI shook her hand. "This must be a worrying time for you?"

Debbie ran a hand through her hair. "It is. This isn't like Kate. It's not like her at all."

Yvonne guided her to a seat in the windowless interview room. "This isn't a formal interview, Debbie... More an informal chat to enable me to know Kate a little better, and understand what is going on in her life."

Taylor placed her shoulder bag down on the floor beside her chair. "Anything I can do to help." She nodded, leaning back in her seat.

"I understand that this is out of character for your friend?"

"Totally, she has never even had a sleepover before."

"Really?" The DI's forehead furrowed.

"I'm serious." Debbie kept her gaze direct. "She always goes home after an evening out."

"When was the last time you saw her?"

"The afternoon she went missing. We had an arts class in the pottery room."

"How did she seem?"

"She was fine. I noticed nothing out of the ordinary. We chatted as we always do."

"I'm told she isn't involved with anyone romantically. Is that true?" Yvonne leaned in, elbows on the table.

"Yes, it is. I think Kate is saving herself for someone special."

"She said that?"

"Well, not in so many words, no. But you can tell from the way she is. She likes romantic forevermore movies, and has never been into one-night-stands."

"I see. What about Stuart Benham? Was she seeing him?"

"Stuart? Not exactly."

"What do you mean, not exactly?"

"He pestered her for ages. She only liked him as a friend. Kate went out with him twice, maybe three times, but made it clear to him they were just friends, and wouldn't be anything more."

"How did he take that?"

"Mostly, he took it okay..."

"What do you mean, mostly?"

"Well..." She bit her lip. "I saw them arguing about a week before Kate disappeared."

"Really?" The DI leaned in. "What was the argument about?"

Debbie shrugged. "I couldn't be sure. It got quite heated,

and Stuart stormed off afterwards, but Kate refused to talk about it. I was in an upstairs window, and I saw them rowing in the carpark. I didn't see Kate again until the following day, and she wouldn't discuss the altercation."

"Did you overhear anything specific? Did you get any of the argument at all?"

"No, I'm afraid I was too far away. I knew they were arguing from their body language, but what it was about is a total mystery to me."

"How was Kate when you saw her the next day?"

"She was quieter than usual, I would say. Lost in her own thoughts."

"Did you ask her specifically about the row?"

"I did, and I tried to make light of things, to encourage her to talk."

"But she wouldn't?"

"Not a word."

"Do you think she may have been protecting Stuart?"

Debbie shrugged. "I don't know... Maybe?"

"Would she normally have talked with you about such things?"

"Yes... Or, at least, she did if she ever argued with her parents, for instance."

"Did she seem out of sorts in the days before she disappeared? Did you witness other tense moments involving her?"

"No, I didn't see her arguing with anyone else, or see her particularly stressed after that row with Stuart. My best guess is he had been pressuring her for a relationship, and she put him in his place."

"In your opinion, would he have taken things further?"

"You mean use force?"

The DI pressed her lips together. "Yes."

"I wouldn't have said so, but I wonder..." Debbie tilted her head, her eyes on the ceiling as though contemplating the possibility. "He'd never gotten physical with anyone before, to my knowledge. But..." She brought her eyes back to the DI. "There's always a first time?"

"Indeed." Yvonne pushed her chair back. "Thank you, Debbie. We'll be in touch."

"You will keep looking for her, won't you?" She asked, rising from the chair.

"Of course." She showed Kate's friend to the door. "We're not planning on giving up."

∽

Yvonne joined Dewi in the office after her interview with Debbie Taylor.

"How did it go?" he asked, setting down his paperwork.

"Kate had a major altercation with Stuart Benham a week before she went missing."

"You've spoken to him, haven't you?" He frowned.

"I did, and he never once mentioned arguing with her."

"Is he hiding something?"

"I don't know, Dewi, but we will find out. I think we'll get him in for a formal interview."

∽

That evening, Yvonne took a mug of Horlicks and Mal's leather notebook to bed, examining his entries which were written in ballpoint and pencil.

Dotted between the names and addresses were often diagrams and schematics, with sparse or abbreviated labels.

These appeared to outline constructions. Some buildings were obvious, such as barns, woodsheds, and storage units. Others were more obscure.

Mal was offering help and advice, and even design ideas, to homeowners and local farmers who wanted outbuildings on their properties.

On arrival at work the following morning, she stated this to Dewi. "I guess it was a win-win for both the store and the client. Garvey-and-Griffiths secured the sale of materials and equipment, and the customer got help and advice with his self-build, with no need for expensive architects."

He looked through the drawings. "I wonder if he helped them with outlines for the council? You know, for the relevant planning permissions?"

"Oh yes, I hadn't thought of that." She frowned. "I think that's something we should investigate. In the meantime, I think we should track down some of those clients and find out what they know. Maybe they'll have pieces of the puzzle for us?"

"If they can remember what was going on seventeen years ago..." He pulled a face.

"I think Mal's disappearance would have cemented events in their memory. They would have been wracking their brains trying to figure out what happened to him."

Dewi nodded. "Which projects was he advising on before he vanished?" He flicked through the book.

"It looks like a barn, a storage facility, and another project I am unsure about." She pointed out the relevant schematics. "This is the one I am unclear about. It's a complex diagram, with a label reading 'air vents'."

Dewi scratched his head. "Some sort of drying facility, maybe? Doesn't look like a kitchen."

"No..." She rubbed her chin. "Unfortunately, the

diagrams are written separately from the relevant names and addresses, so we will have to rely on the customers telling us what these drawings are, and which project they were connected to."

"How is this related to his murder?" Dewi tilted his head.

"I don't know if it is, but Mal's life revolved around his work and family. So, our investigative efforts must revolve around those, too."

"Sure..." The DS nodded. "I'll get on with tracing the customers named in this book. I think I know at least one of them."

"Brilliant, Dewi. Let me know when you've located them."

"Will do."

∽

SALIM ABADEH ARRIVED for the interview of Reza Hassani, casually dressed in a yellow polo shirt and chinos.

Yvonne wondered at the interpreter's change of style as she showed him to the interview room, explaining that Hassani had yet to show. She read through her notes, while he busied himself with work from his briefcase, until a PC knocked on the door and showed Hassani in.

The DI pointed the twenty-five-year-old to the chair next to Abadeh. "Thank you for coming in to talk to us," she began.

The young interviewee was attired in tee-shirt and jeans, as his friend Ahmed had been, except Hassani's footwear was clean. His hair was as dark as his friends, but shorter, and he had a moustache but no beard. His dark eyes held a hint of defiance.

The Bunker Murders

Salim hastily replaced papers into his briefcase, ready to translate Yvonne's words.

The DI cleared her throat as Reza's strong aftershave hit the back of it. "Do you know why you're here?" she asked, her voice soft, eyes studying his face.

"No."

She frowned. "Did your friend Ahmed not speak to you last night?"

He clasped his hands together on the table, saying nothing.

"Very well." Yvonne pushed forward the first of the photographs of Kate. "Do you recognise this girl, Reza?"

"No." He shook his head. "Sorry."

"What about now?" She pushed forward the CCTV still image of Kate in her cycling gear, the one taken on the afternoon of her disappearance.

He licked his lips, colour rising in his cheeks. He ran a hand through his hair. "Yes, I think I recognise her now." Sweat appeared on his temples.

"Where have you seen her before?"

Hassani had a brief exchange with the interpreter.

Yvonne waited.

"He says he saw her cycling by the river last week."

"Did you talk to her?"

Further exchange with the Abadeh.

"No, he didn't."

"Did you try to? Did you approach her at all?"

The interpreter answered. "He says he did not approach her."

Hassani shifted position in his chair, rubbing his knuckles. The middle one on his right hand was bruised and swollen.

Yvonne's gaze lingered on that knuckle long enough for him to become aware.

He covered it with his left hand.

"Hmm..." She rubbed her chin, pushing forward the photograph of Reza and Ahmed on the wall, watching Kate on her bicycle. "This young woman is Kate Hughes. She is missing. Can you remember what you were talking about on that wall?"

Hassani shrugged. "No."

"You were talking while watching her. This image is from our CCTV footage."

Hassani waited for Abadeh to translate before he answered for himself. "Just chat. Nothing special."

"Did Ahmed speak to Kate?"

"No."

"I understand you are applying for asylum?" She changed the subject.

"I no get a passport. My mum is sick. She misses me. I want go back to Iraq for visit."

"I see-"

"Also, I want work. I have no money. I help my friend in kebab shop, but cannot have money."

"You mean you can't be paid?"

"Yes, no pay for us."

"How are you buying food?"

Hassani discussed with the interpreter, who answered.

"He says he has kind friends who provide food and somewhere to stay. He says he doesn't know what he would do without them."

"I see... Are you eating regularly?"

Reza would not make eye contact with her, yet he appeared to have no trouble doing so with his male interpreter.

The DI was unsure whether this was merely a cultural issue. "Mister Hassani, what is the name of your landlord? The man whose house you are staying in?"

Another exchange between the two men.

"Amir... Amir Khan. He drive taxi."

"He's a taxi driver?'

"Yes... taxi driver."

"How long have you been living with Amir Khan?"

Hassani didn't answer.

Yvonne had this information already, having checked with immigration. She knew about the failed asylum attempts and the fake education credentials they used to gain student visas. Both Hassani and Syeed were on borrowed time for their stay in the UK. Perhaps Khan had felt sorry for them, taken them in out of the goodness of his heart.

She continued, pointing to his damaged knuckle. "What happened to your hand?"

He covered it once more. "Is nothing."

"How did you get that bruise? It doesn't look like nothing?"

"I got mad. I hit wall." His eyes met hers. They narrowed, communicating dislike.

"What made you so angry you hit a wall?" She cocked her head.

"I don't remember."

"Did you have an argument with someone? Did something happen?"

"I don't remember."

"Your hand is badly swollen. Surely you remember why you hurt it like that?"

He refused to answer.

"Very well. I don't think we can take this any further

today. However, should you decide to talk to me, and if you remember interacting with Kate Hughes, call us or call into the station? Be warned, if you had anything to do with the disappearance of this girl, we will find out. Better you talk to us before that."

His scowl of contempt was her only reply.

11

THE SCRUFFY VAN

"Ma'am..." DC Dai Clayton caught up with her in the corridor. "We got CCTV footage of the white van that was parked in Llanllwchaiarn on the afternoon of Kate Hughes' disappearance."

"Great... I thought there were no cameras operational on that stretch of the towpath?"

"We got it from the driver of a Luton van that was parked behind it the day before. Now, we don't know for sure that it is the same van, but probably it is as the witnesses only saw one such van on the two days and were sure it was the same one."

"Okay, what do we know about it?"

"It's a Ford Transit, owned by one Amir Khan, who drives taxis for a living. He was working for a Newtown firm, but switched to working for himself on private hire."

"He's the landlord of the two Iraqi men I've just interviewed, the guys who watched her from the wall."

"Yes, well apparently, Amir Khan also operates a cash-in-hand courier service for locals who wish to move furniture, takeaways, and parcels around. He doesn't advertise, but relies heavily on word-of-mouth to get business."

"Does he indeed?" She pursed her lips, mulling over the connection.

"I thought we could speak to him today, so I phoned him, and he said he will be at his property in Commercial Street between two and three this afternoon."

"Great... Good work, Dai. You can come with me if you have the time?"

"Yep, no worries. I'll let Callum know he'll be on his own this afternoon."

Yvonne frowned in concentration. "The coincidences in this case keep on stacking up."

∽

AMIR KHAN STOOD in the doorway of his mid-terrace, Georgian town house, smoking a rolled-up cigarette.

He motioned Yvonne and Dai in before blowing the last puff of smoke into the air, stubbing the butt out with his fingers, and tossing it into his tiny garden.

They followed him through a narrow hallway, into a small open-plan lounge and galley kitchen that smelled of fried food and cigarettes.

He pointed to a sagging green-fabric couch. "Please, take a seat."

"Thank you for agreeing to see us," Yvonne began, taking out her notebook. "I know you have a busy schedule as a taxi driver."

She thought at first he would not answer. He had his back to them, running a discoloured dishcloth over the kitchen counter, and muttering something inaudible. She got the feeling he was complaining about the cleanliness of his lodgers.

Finally, he turned to them. "I have to go out again at three."

"We know." The DI levelled a cool gaze at him, noting his English was excellent. "Do you have any other work besides driving taxis, Amir?"

"No." He turned away again, fiddling with something in the sink.

"Really? I thought you ran errands for people in your van."

His shoulders stiffened. "For friends," he answered, without turning round.

"They pay you, don't they?" she pressed.

He swivelled towards her, eyes cold. "They give me money for fuel used for the journey."

"You mean you don't declare it?" Dai chimed in. "No proper records?"

"Why did you want to talk to me? I don't do many trips in the van. I'm too busy with the taxi."

Yvonne pulled out the photographs of Kate Hughes, and held up two side-by-side, showing her with and without cycle gear. "Do you recognise this young woman?"

Khan approached her to peer at the images. "No, I have never seen her before."

"Are you sure? Take another look," she instructed as he pulled away.

"I'm sure I would have remembered her." He flicked his head in dismissal.

"Do you have family here, Amir?"

"No, my wife left three years ago, when we lived in Wolverhampton. She went back to Pakistan."

"I see. Are you seeing anyone?"

"No time for that," he snapped.

She continued, keeping her eyes on his face. "The young woman in these photos is Kate Hughes. She disappeared last Wednesday afternoon after leaving college."

"What has that got to do with me?" He rubbed the back of his neck.

"We have CCTV footage of her journey home that day. We have her cycling along the river, and then along the canal towpath."

He swallowed.

The DI held up more photos. "This is her riding along the towpath. We found her bike in the canal, cleaned of any fingerprints, including her own."

"So, why are you talking to me?"

She handed him a further image. "Do you recognise the white van in that image?"

He swallowed again.

"Now you know why we are talking to you?"

He scowled. "What is this? You think I kidnapped this girl in my van? Is that what you are trying to say?"

"Why was your van there, Amir? Were you there? Were you driving the van that day?"

"I can't remember. I drive many places, dropping people and goods off."

"This isn't your taxi, it's your van. You said you move people's things for them out of the goodness of your heart. Are you telling me now you cannot remember helping someone only last week?"

"I've made a lot of journeys since then. I don't know... Maybe I dropped someone's parcel there."

"Did you, or didn't you? Surely, not that difficult to recall?"

"It may have been a parcel drop off. I help local couriers

sometimes, doing an afternoon of deliveries at short notice, if their driver calls in sick. I can give you the number of the company. You can check with them."

"I will." She handed him her pen. "And the names and business addresses, please."

He scribbled on a notepad next to the phone, tore off the page, and passed it to her. "I had nothing to do with the disappearance of the girl."

"Your van was seen on two consecutive afternoons prior to Kate going missing, according to a local resident. Each time, you parked in the same spot."

He shrugged. "Many deliveries have to be signed for. If I cannot deliver one day, I might have to go back the next."

"So, two afternoons attempting to deliver to the same address in Llanllwchaiarn, and you don't remember?"

"I remember being there now. I can't remember the name or number of the house. And I wouldn't know what was in the parcel."

"Why can't you remember the address?"

"What Three Words." He smirked.

"Sorry?"

"It's an app. The address is three words decided by the app and the address owner. I used the app to go directly to the doorstep."

"I see." She pursed her lips. "I will speak to the courier firm to verify what you have told me."

"Go ahead." He yawned, making a point of looking at his watch. "I really have to go out now, officers."

She resisted the urge to carry on pushing, glancing at Dai. "I think we're about done here. Thank you, Amir. We'll be in touch."

∼

"He's not declaring those earnings, is he?" Dai pulled a face as they left the house on Commercial Street.

"No, he isn't. I wonder what other dodgy dealings he has going on? Can you look into it for me, Dai? I'm wondering if we have people-trafficking going on here. He may or may not be telling us the truth, but I still believe he is hiding something."

"Will do." Dai nodded. "And, I agree. He's not telling us everything he knows."

"While you are at it, could you speak to the courier firm for me?" She handed him the paper given to her by Khan. "Look into this firm and find out if they agree with his story. Keep a healthy scepticism. We don't know what they may be involved in."

"On it..." He unlocked the car. "What are you going to do?"

"I'm hoping Dewi has some addresses for me for some of Malcolm Edwards' old clients, the ones he was dealing with before he was murdered. I'm hoping to pay them a visit. If one of them murdered him, they'll be feeling fraught now his remains have been found. I want to apply a little pressure, see what gives..."

12

VICTIM'S SHOES

Dewi held a sheaf of paper, a broad smile on his face, chest puffed out.

"You look happy..." Yvonne couldn't help grinning back. "What have you got for me?"

"Three names and addresses, all clients of Mal's, with active accounts at the time Mal was killed."

"Wow, you have been busy..." She accepted the papers. "This is excellent, Dewi. Are they local?"

He nodded. "They are. The furthest is living thirty-three miles away in Llanfyllin. Two of them have moved since Mal's time, but one still lives at the same address... a farm near Caersws."

"Okay, great, I'll have a look through these and we'll go talk to them. Find out more about Mal and his work, and why he was so prepared to go the extra mile for them."

Dewi nodded. "Let me know when you are ready, and I'll set up a meeting with them."

∽

She sat with the details of Wyn Thomas, Bryn Ellis, and David Cadman provided by her sergeant.

Wyn Thomas ran an inherited dairy farm off the road to Caersws, five miles south-west of Newtown. His family had farmed there for more than a century.

Bryn Ellis was living in a bungalow in Aberhafesp, two miles south of Newtown, but had lived in a detached home on the Milford Road during Mal's time.

David Cadman had moved from a house on Canal Road to Llanfyllin and was currently living furthest away.

All three had meetings with Mal in the last weeks of his life, seeking help and advice with their home projects.

The drawings in Mal's notebook were likely linked to at least some of their endeavours.

Yvonne was sure she would learn more about his work from them, and perhaps a motive for his murder. A greater understanding of who and what he was would be key, she was sure.

∽

Stuart Benham attended the station in the same clothes he wore when meeting her previously at the college.

She hoped they had been washed in the meantime, even though he was across the table from her. "Thanks for coming in, Stuart. I know how much you worry about your peers' perceptions."

"I'm worried about Kate," he said, while leaning back in his chair, legs outstretched and crossed at the ankles. His hands rested in his jeans pockets.

"Hmm." Yvonne pressed her lips together. "Have you heard from her? What are people saying on campus?"

Benham shrugged. "I have heard nothing." He licked his

upper lip, taking his hands out of his pockets to drum his fingers on the legs of his chair.

"When we spoke the other day, you told me you took Kate's refusal of your kiss and date well. Do you remember telling me that?"

"Yeah." He looked at her from beneath the hair falling over his face.

"We've had conflicting information since then, Stuart."

"What do you mean?" He folded his arms, flicking his head to remove the hair from his eyes, revealing acne spots which he had picked until they bled.

"We have a witness who says they saw you rowing with Kate in the days before she disappeared."

"Debbie Taylor," he blurted.

"Sorry?" The DI frowned.

"I'll bet your witness is Debbie Taylor." He scowled. "Well... she would say that, wouldn't she?"

"Why do you assume it was Debbie who told us?"

"She doesn't like me."

"Why? Why doesn't she like you?"

"She used to be interested in me, but I was only interested in Kate. She propositioned me, you know?"

Yvonne scratched her head. "That's quite a tangled picture you are painting, Stuart."

He shrugged.

"When you say she proportioned you, what do you mean? In what way?"

"A group of her friends were going to a local pub, and she asked me if I would like to go with them."

"Well, that's not exactly a proposition, Stuart. She may simply have wanted to be friendly."

"I didn't get the impression she was just being nice. She

wanted more. I turned her down, and her attitude towards me changed."

"I see... So, are you telling me there was no row between yourself and Kate in the days prior to her disappearance?"

"Yes, that is what I am saying."

"What about when she refused your kiss?"

"I may have tried to persuade her a little-"

"Persuade her, how?"

"Talk her into it, you know..."

"I don't know. I wasn't there." The DI felt her patience waning. "How did she react?"

"I told you, she pushed me away."

"And how did you react?"

"I tried apologising the following day at college."

"Was that in the carpark?"

He scoured her face. "Yes."

"How did she take the apology?"

"She got annoyed... Accused me of pestering. I told her I wasn't that desperate."

"Is that when you stormed off?"

"How did you know?" His eyes narrowed. "Yes, I left. I was offended. Anyone would have been in my shoes."

"Did you speak to her again after that?"

"No."

"Maybe on the towpath?"

"No." He shouted. Then glanced around at the PC by the door. "I haven't harmed Kate, if that is where this is going? You think I did something to her? Prove it. You won't... You can't, because I did nothing."

She kept her voice calm. "I'm a police officer. We ask questions. Sometimes, those questions are tough to answer, but we still ask. It's our job. You want to know where Kate is, don't you?"

"Yes, of course I do." He pulled a face.

"Well then, I'm asking hard questions of everybody in her inner circle. She deserves no less."

His shoulders dropped. "Fine... I'm sorry."

"That's all right, everybody's tense." She tilted her head. "Did you see her at all on the day she disappeared?"

"I saw her through the window, but not to talk to." He sighed. "I really wish I had gotten to speak with her. I wonder if it would have made a difference." He stared at his hands on the table.

"She may still turn up?" Yvonne narrowed her eyes.

"Yes, of course." He didn't look up.

13

CLIENTS

Wyn Thomas's dairy farm abutted the main road into Caersws, and was entered via a gate next to two enormous tanks, like upright bullets, with ladders up their sides.

He waited for them as they parked up. Wearing navy-blue overalls with rolled-up sleeves, and wellingtons caked in slurry, he looked every inch the farmer.

Yvonne estimated him to be mid-fifties. When he spoke, it was with a pronounced Welsh accent. She suspected English was a second language, though he used it well.

"You found me all right, then?"

She smiled. "DI Yvonne Giles, and this is DS Dewi Hughes." She held out her hand.

He looked at his own, checking it was clean enough, before accepting the handshake.

"Wyn Thomas, I'm the farmer." His hand was warm but rough from exposure to the weather and manual work. He sniffed and grunted to clear his congested nose and throat. "Follow me. I think we had better go over to the house. You'll get cold standing there."

Yvonne wasn't about to argue with him. The chill had already stiffened the muscles between her shoulder blades. She wiped her nose with a hanky. "Yes, inside would be good."

Dewi appeared comfortable in his long black overcoat, thick scarf, and black leather gloves.

She wished she too had thought to bring a scarf and gloves, but had left that morning in a hurry, and without Tasha reminding her to take them.

They followed Thomas towards the Welsh-slated stone farmhouse.

He kicked his boots off on the front porch. "Got to keep the wife happy." He grinned. "Would you like tea?"

Wyn led them into the welcoming warmth of the kitchen, where a cream-coloured Aga belted out heat from under a Tudor fireplace, and filled the kettle. He placed it on the boiler-plate, where its wet bottom sizzled, while he grabbed three mugs from a wooden tree on the countertop. "So, how can I help you? I understand you want to talk to me about Mal?"

"That's right..." Yvonne nodded, her eyes on the chipped rim of the nearest mug, as he poured the tea.

He handed it to her. "There's milk and sugar in front of you." He pulled out the chairs for them to sit at the formica-covered table, the middle of which held a huddle of condiments, the milk jug, and a bowl of sugar covered in a doily of white lace.

The DI added a trickle of milk to her mug, sipping at it left-handed, to avoid the cleft in the rim. "You received help from Mal for a project you were working on in the weeks before he went missing?"

"That was a terrible business," he said, shaking his head. "Them finding his bones like that. I couldn't believe it when

I saw it on the telly. I mean, I thought it was very odd when he vanished, like. But I didn't think..." His voice trailed away as he ran a hand through sandy hair peppered with grey.

"You didn't think he'd been murdered?" Dewi finished the sentence for him.

"No..." Wyn scratched his head. "It never entered my head."

"Did you think him the sort to run away?" Yvonne tilted her head. "Would he have had reason to do that?"

"There was some heavy rivalry between the stores back then."

"Which stores?"

"Well... We only have one Garvey-and-Griffiths now but, back then, there were three of them, and all were thriving businesses. The head office gave out a hefty bonus each year as incentive for staff to build good relations with the customer base."

"Do you mean Christmas cash bonuses?"

"Yes, the store with the highest sales each year got a decent bonus for the highest achieving staff member. The other staff at that store didn't get bonuses, but I think they got their Christmas meals paid for."

"Did Mal tell you that?"

"I don't remember him mentioning it, but it was common knowledge back then, the newspapers always printed the name of the winning store and staff member."

"I see." Yvonne pursed her lips. "So a staff member such as Mal might go the extra mile to help their store and themselves win the company competition?"

Thomas nodded. "I reckon it would have played a part, yes."

"How did you get on with Mal personally?"

"Me?" Wyn shrugged. "I got on with him all right. We

The Bunker Murders

didn't always see eye-to-eye on some parts of a project, but he always seemed a decent bloke to me."

"Which jobs did he advise you on? What were your projects?"

"Well, let's see now... I gotta think about this. I'd done a few with him, over the years."

"Take as much time as you need."

"There was the barn in the west field. That required a new building when it was wrecked by fire. Everything went up. We had bales in there for the animals... We lost the lot." He shook his head. "The insurance money was a while in coming, so we used what little spare money we had to buy in feed pellets and more bales. We rebuilt ourselves, and that's where Mal's help and advice came in handy. He was great, helping us with the design as well as choosing the best materials. He helped us comply with building regulations, too. We needed that. The fire had been devastating. We had a few things go wrong all at once, and the wife and I actually cried when the barn went up. We wondered what else life could throw at us. Anyway, in comes Mal with his thinking cap on, and he made us feel better right away. He told us what we needed, and how we could get it at the best cost. We'd cut right back on labour, see. I did a lot of the work myself, with some help from my brother."

"Okay..." The DI scratched her chin. "Besides the barn, Wyn, did you have other work done? And did Mal help with it?"

"Little bits and pieces in the farmhouse. I think we had some cupboards built in, that sort of thing. Mal gave us advice on the materials, but not style or anything. Really, it was only the barn... I think."

Yvonne pulled out a photocopy of the room plan she had found in Mal's leather book, the diagram with very few labels. "Do you recognise this?" She tilted her head, studying the farmer's face.

He shook his head, frowning. "No, I can't say I do. What is it?"

"I don't know." She pursed her lips. "It was drawn by Mal before he died."

"Oh, I see. Do you think it had something to do with his murder, then?"

"I don't know." She showed him another of Mal's drawings. "Was this the plan of your barn?"

He leaned in. "I think it could be. Looks similar to the barn, and I think I've seen that drawing before... Must have been when Mal showed it to me all those years ago."

She pencilled a note on the photocopy. "Thank you, Wyn." She put the drawings away. "Were you aware of anyone wanting to harm Mal?"

He shook his head. "No, not at all."

"What about now? Have you heard anything since that made you suspicious?"

"No."

"You said there were rivalries between staff at the Garvey-and-Griffiths stores?"

His forehead creased. "I said there was competition for the bonuses. I don't know of anyone who would have killed in order to get a bonus. It would seem extreme, like." He wiped his forehead with a hanky. "Then again, who knows? There are some strange folk out there."

"All right, Wyn." She rose from her seat, giving a nod to Dewi. "I think that will be all for now. Thank you for your time."

"No problem..." He rose to see them out. "I hope you find Mal's murderer. He deserves that, at least."

"We'll do our best." She turned back to him before they

reached the door. "If you hear anything you think is relevant, please call us."

"I will."

As they left, Yvonne pondered the new information regarding Garvey-and-Griffiths bonuses. Could these have been a motive for murder? Mal's colleagues mentioned no such payments. Perhaps, she reasoned, it might be worth speaking with them again.

∼

Bryn Ellis's cream-rendered bungalow was on the south side of the Aberhafesp hamlet, with sweeping views over the undulating Welsh landscape.

Yvonne took in the scenery as Dewi retrieved his jacket from the boot of the car. She filled her lungs and thought of Tasha, the birdsong ringing in her ears.

"You coming, then?" Dewi asked, grinning at her faraway look. "Some of us have work to do."

"Sorry, Dewi." Her mind came back to the present, and she pulled her coat tight around her. For all its beauty, the day held a penetrating chill.

Dewi led them through the gate, and along a wood chip pathway to the front door. He gave it two sharp raps.

It was opened by a six-foot male, around fifty years of age, with short grey hair. When he smiled, a pronounced gap was visible between his two front teeth. "You must be DI Giles," he said, addressing Dewi.

"Er, no... I'm DS Hughes." He turned to Yvonne. "This is DI Giles."

"Oh God, I'm sorry." Ellis coloured. "Trust me to put my foot in-"

She held up a hand. "It's okay. I'm not at all bothered. It's a simple mistake to make."

"Phew," he said with another toothy grin. "Come in. My wife is just in the kitchen making tea. You've come at the right time. I'm taking a break from the office. One perk of working from home, being able to rearrange your rest periods to suit."

"What is it you do, Mister Ellis?"

"Bryn, please... Doesn't seem right you calling me Mister. I sell merchandise online, some to local businesses, and the rest all round the country and places abroad. People buy items with our designs on or with their own brands, whichever suits. My daughter Melanie studied graphic art at university, so most of the artwork is hers. I photograph local wildlife and such, which is popular with overseas markets."

"I see. It must keep you busy?"

"It does, and my daughter lives away. We catch up on Zoom or Messenger. We have a couple of meetings a week. This is my wife, Elyn," he said as they reached the kitchen.

Mrs Ellis poured water into a sizeable stainless steel teapot, greeting them as they entered. "Nice to meet you. Come in, you must be cold." Her hair was a mussed ginger, which she pushed behind her ears to keep it out of her face. Shee had freckles and high cheekbones. "Would you like tea?" she asked, pulling mugs down from a cupboard.

"That would be lovely, thank you." The DI, feeling chilled all morning, would be grateful for the warming liquid.

"You came to talk to us about Mal Edwards?" Bryn accepted a cup of tea from his wife.

"Yes." Yvonne took a seat at the round table. "You may have heard about his remains being discovered in the fields recently. He was murdered."

The Bunker Murders

"I heard..." He turned his face towards the window. "Do you know how he died?" He cleared his throat.

Yvonne thought she caught a tremor in his voice. "He was stabbed in his chest and stomach." Her eyes were on the side of Bryn's face.

He shuddered. "Oh, God."

Elyn's teacup rattled on her saucer.

"Do you know anything about his death?" Yvonne's voice was soft as she observed their body language.

"No... Why should we? We barely knew him." He shrugged, turning back to the officers. "I asked his advice when I went to Garvey-and-Griffiths, and he helped me with ideas for the building of our art studio, the one we created at our previous house. We knew very little about his personal life. I mean, he was a nice guy to us... really helpful. I can't for the life of me think of a reason anyone would want him dead. When he disappeared, I thought he'd had an accident somewhere or committed suicide and hadn't been found. He didn't seem a man someone would murder." Bryn's eyes met his wife's. "I'd forgotten all about it until now."

"How often did you visit the store?" The DI tilted her head.

"Oh, I was a regular there at one time, mostly while we were constructing the art studio as an extension of the house."

"Did you work with a builder or only with Mal?"

"We had a builder, initially. It didn't work out, though. Our finances were tight back then, and I went it alone after the foundations were laid. That's where Mal and his invaluable advice came in."

"I understand there were three Garvey-and-Griffiths stores in those days?"

"There were, and I went to the others once or twice

when the Newtown warehouse didn't have what I needed. The other stores closed during the financial crash that began in two-thousand-eight. They were in Welshpool and Llanidloes."

"I see. Were you aware of any tensions between staff or between stores?"

"No, I didn't hear of anything." He frowned. "After Mal went missing, I read an article in the local newspaper about staff bonuses, and the competition between them all, but to be honest, I think it may have been a sinister spin to sell more copy rather than truth."

"You didn't get the sense that Mal was ambitious?"

"I think Mal was a nice guy who enjoyed helping people. If that got him an extra Christmas bonus, or helped his store receive extra benefits? Well, that is all to the good. He worked hard, he deserved it."

"Did he ever discuss his life outside of work with you? Was he worried about anyone? Did he sense danger?"

"I remember nothing like that. I doubt he would have told me, anyway. He was a professional. If he had worries, he kept them to himself. Mal was always focussed on the work."

She pulled the photocopies out of her bag. "Bryn, these are sketches Mal made in his notebooks. I think they are ideas for projects he was helping with. The diagrams were probably done to help him remember. Do you recognise any? Do you know what these projects were? Could one of them have been a design for your art studio?"

Bryn screwed his eyes up, holding the plan at arm's length. "Hang on, I'll grab my specs..." He retrieved them from a wooden case on the table, and rotated the drawings left and right. "Well, this one looks like the plan of a room, but it's not the art studio he helped us with." He ran a hand through his hair.

"You're sure of that?"

"Yes, this is a square space, and our studio was an octagonal design of mostly glass. This is not something we designed together."

"I see. Thank you for clearing that up for us."

"He was missed, you know... Mal was one of a kind. He was a good man. People speculated about his death for months after he disappeared. I know search parties scoured the countryside for weeks. The community cared about him."

"We know he was well-liked."

"Search teams went over that ground."

"Which ground?" Yvonne raised a brow.

"Where his remains were found. They had sticks and dogs, the works. I am sure I saw pictures of them in those fields on the Welsh news and in the County Times."

"And all the while, he was supposedly up there in a shallow grave." She narrowed her eyes.

"Exactly... Why didn't they find him? Perhaps, Inspector, he wasn't there?"

"Hmm." She considered this possibility as she replaced the photocopies in her bag, rising from her seat. "Thank you for your time, Bryn." She nodded to his wife. "Elyn."

"You're welcome," he answered. "Any time."

As they left, Yvonne turned to Dewi. "Perhaps Mal wasn't killed right away?"

He nodded. "Or his body was moved to the fields from some other location?"

"Like he was buried or stored somewhere else and moved when things became too hot?"

"Exactly... I think we have to keep digging."

She nodded. "I want to speak to Mal's wife again. Even if he wasn't overly ambitious, his colleagues may have been. Perhaps he discussed it with Rhiannon."

"I thought she told you he had no enemies?"

"I'll ask her about rivalries, specifically. It might spark a memory."

"Got it." He opened the car door. "Let's go talk to David Cadman," he said, referring to the last client of Mal's on their list. "See what he has got to say?"

∼

It took them almost an hour to cover the thirty-five miles to Cadman's detached home in Llanfyllin.

They found the fifty-five-year-old in his garden, enjoying early retirement with a cafetiere of coffee under a cherry tree. The chill of the morning air having given way to a warm afternoon with a light breeze.

"Mister Cadman?" Yvonne called, as they traversed the flagstone path through the freshly trimmed garden surrounded by copper beech hedges.

"That's me..." He looked up from his newspaper, his movements slow and relaxed as he leaned back in his recliner.

"DI Yvonne Giles and DS Dewi Hughes."

Cadman checked his watch. "And right on time." He pushed tinted glasses to the top of his head.

She suspected he worked out, or maybe it was garden maintenance that kept him lean. The DI estimated him to be six feet as he rose to shake each of them by the hand.

"Please, take a seat. Would you like coffee? It's freshly ground."

Since he had the extra mugs on hand, they accepted.

Birdsong emanated from every corner. Her eyes wandered over the shrubs and well-kept lawn, wondering how he kept everything so weed-free.

"You wanted to talk to me about Mal Edwards?" He eyed her, his fingers stroking the handle of his coffee mug.

She shifted in her seat, suspecting this was a man who liked control. "I hear you're retired? It must be nice to relax out here on a day like this?"

"It is..." A line of confusion creased his forehead.

She cleared her throat. "We are here to discuss Mal. His remains were found two weeks ago, and I am told you sought his help with a self build project in the last few weeks of his life."

He slowly cupped his hands together, resting his chin on the tips of his fingers. "That's right, I believe I did. I'd planned a large garage-come-workshop, but had limited space available and my budget was tight. I sought Mal's advice regarding the best materials for my money, and how I could heat it effectively as it wouldn't be connected to the house. Mal was great. He helped me choose what I needed from Garvey-and-Griffiths, and showed me where to order the rest from. I planned to build it with my brother Carl, but didn't get around to it until later."

"And this was at your old house on Canal Road in Newtown?"

"Yes, that is correct."

Off to their right, stood a two-storey concrete build, around twenty-five feet square, with windows on each floor and a stairway along the side wall to the top. She turned back to him. "You built it here?"

"I did." He nodded. "I have more room here, albeit the garden is a bit of an odd shape." He pointed to the end of the garden, where the space narrowed to a triangular tip filled with wildflowers and grasses. "I've never known what to do with that part, so I leave it to the wildlife. But I now have my workshop and a garden I can relax in." He ran a hand over cropped grey-blonde hair. "I have good views over the fields. I'm happy."

He looked content, lounging in a short-sleeved linen shirt and casual trousers. Yvonne took the photocopies from her bag. "Do you recognise any of these sketches?"

He accepted them from her, examining each but lingering on the one for which they had not yet found the connection.

"Does that one ring any bells?" She leaned in.

He pursed his lips, pushing it away from him. "No."

"Are you sure?" She raised a brow.

"Yes, I'm sure."

Her eyes travelled to the workshop. "Does your workshop have air vents?"

He nodded. "It does... They're called windows."

She felt the blood rise in her cheeks, mentally cursing them for their betrayal of her embarrassment. "May we see inside?"

"Sure..." He rose from his seat. "Come on, I'll show you around."

They followed him into the concrete building.

"Wow," she said. "It's a Tardis inside, so much bigger than it looks from out there. It's so modern."

"It is. I think the straight lines and the stairs in the wall leading to the mezzanine give it that vibe."

Her eyes followed the steps, which lacked a handrail. They looked like they were growing organically from the wall.

"I do a spot of metal- and woodworking in my spare

time," he added. "I make a bit of extra cash selling bits to my friends."

Yvonne noted the large machinery along the wall opposite.

"I reckon it's a nuclear shelter, you know?"

"Sorry?" She frowned.

"The diagram you showed me. The build with air vents. It may be someone's bomb shelter."

"Really?" She scratched her chin. "Well, that would make sense. I guess. Do you know of anyone who has one?"

He shook his head. "No, but you could make enquiries with the council. The owner most likely sought planning permission." He shrugged. "It's just an idea."

"Thank you for the suggestion." He had a point, and she realised the building they were in was not the construction sketched out in Mal's leather notebook. Perhaps Cadman had hit the nail on the head, and Mal had been helping somebody build a bomb shelter.

14

THE WOMEN WHO VANISHED

"Kate Hughes' disappearance may be linked to other women who vanished." Dai waved three manilla folders at her as she and Dewi arrived back at the station.

"Meaning?" She threw her coat over the back of her chair.

He slapped the folders onto her desk. "Meaning, I've found at least three similar disappearances going back fifteen years, the earliest of which was two-thousand-seven."

"No way?" She grabbed the files. "Tell me what you've got."

"Three disappearances of young women near waterways. Two of them were said to have been riding their bikes at the time they vanished. The third female was on foot, and they couldn't be sure that she had made it as far as the river, there being no witnesses who saw her."

"Okay..."

"The most recent case was Kelly Lewis. She was nineteen when she disappeared while riding her bike along the river in Welshpool, in two-thousand-seventeen."

"Kelly Lewis, that case rings a bell. It wasn't one we worked on."

"No... The second case is that of Nina Richards, disappeared aged eighteen while cycling along the river in Llanidloes in two-thousand-twelve. And the third, Mair Harris, twenty-two, had intended cycling along the canal at Newtown in August two-thousand-seven. She wasn't seen again, and the bike was never found. There was no CCTV for her journey, so they couldn't say whether she had made it as far as the towpath."

"Four disappearances, each with five years between, wow... Could we be looking at a serial offender? Well done, Dai. Track down everything you can in connection to those disappearances, including CCTV if any still exists. I'll look through these MisPer files, see if anything else links these disappearances."

"Right-oh, ma'am." Dai nodded. "I'll get on."

~

It was past seven when Yvonne left the office, her head filled with the details of the three possibly related cases found by Dai.

No bodies had ever been recovered and, as with Kate Hughes, friends and family had reported the absences as being unexpected and out of character. Because the girls were cycling near rivers, it was thought they had fallen into the water, and drowned. But the similarity to Kate Hughes's disappearance was striking.

Five years was a long cooling off time for a serial offender, but longer had been known. If these girls were abducted, they may subsequently have been murdered. Their abductor would almost certainly have been local, since Newtown, Llanidloes, and Welshpool were all within a thirty-mile radius, the centre point of which was Newtown.

She had pointed this out to Dewi before leaving the station, and before taking the missing girls' files home with her. Although officially still open, it had been some time since anyone had doggedly worked the Nina Richards and Mair Harris cases. An officer from Welshpool was still working the Kelly Lewis case, but only a few hours a week, and he was on desk duty due to injuring his legs in a road traffic collision in two-thousand-eighteen. DC Wayne Collison now worked in a back office at the tiny Welshpool Station. Perhaps she would pay him a visit later in the week.

As she pulled into her yard, Yvonne noticed the lights were on in the house. "Tasha," she said, her face breaking into a smile.

The psychologist met her in the hallway, taking her bag and coat to hang on the peg. "Thought I would surprise you." She grinned. "Dinner is cooking."

The DI sniffed the air. "Tagliatelle?" she asked, throwing her arms around her partner. "I've missed you."

"I've missed you too." Tasha led the way through the hall. "I've got a few days free. Now I have completed a profile for our case." She grimaced. "They need me back next week, though. The Met are setting up a sting for the killer."

Yvonne sighed. "Ah well, at least I have you for the next few days."

"Absolutely..." The psychologist poured the wine. "I want to know everything you've been up to."

15

MOTIVES FOR MURDER

Yvonne saw Mal's widow on her own this time.

They knew her husband had not taken out a life insurance policy, and there was little to suggest Rhiannon had any other motive for causing him harm. The DI was more interested in discussing what Mrs Edwards knew of Garvey-and-Griffiths.

Rhiannon talked to her in the galley kitchen. "There was competition for bonuses," she confirmed. "Mal mentioned it a few times. We were always hoping to benefit from a little extra at Christmas. Who doesn't? But I don't think Mal took it as seriously as some of his colleagues."

"Which colleagues?" Yvonne pulled out her notebook.

Rhiannon looked at her hands. "Er... Simon, I think. I'm sure I heard Mal say he was getting worked up about it."

"Would that be Simon Jones?"

Mrs Edwards nodded. "He and Don both wanted recognition more than Mal. My husband was always philosophical about it, even when we were short of money. He used to say if we got the bonus, great. If we didn't? Well, there was no harm done. He believed he would get it if he was meant to, and wouldn't if he wasn't."

"I see..."

"He got a bonus three years running, starting two-thousand-one."

"Did he?" Yvonne rubbed her chin, thinking to herself that he had disappeared before having the chance to win it again in two-thousand-five. She kept this thought to herself. "How much was the bonus in two-thousand-four?"

"Two thousand pounds." Rhiannon sighed. "He was so pleased he could give me the extra cash for the celebrations. I don't remember him keeping any for himself. That's the sort of man he was."

"Did he tell you how the others reacted to him winning that bonus?"

Mrs Edwards shook her head. "He said Simon spoke little for the following few days, and that he and Don would go quiet when Mal walked into the office when they were together."

"Did they?" Yvonne tapped her pen on her lips.

"It's not as though they went without reward..." Rhiannon frowned. "The store from which the winning staff member came got their Christmas meal paid for by head office, no matter the restaurant. Simon and Don both benefitted from that. I don't know how they felt about Mal winning the bonus several years in a row, but my guess is they would have been disappointed." Her widening eyes met the DI's. "You don't think they would have killed him because of the money, do you?"

"At this stage in our investigation, we're not ruling anything out." Yvonne pursed her lips.

"No..." Rhiannon lowered her gaze.

"But it would seem unlikely."

Mrs Edwards appeared satisfied by this. "A bonus is not equivalent to someone's life."

"I would like to think that." The DI readied herself to leave. "Rhiannon, did Mal ever seem afraid of anyone? A colleague or work client?"

She shook her head. "I don't think so."

"Would he have told you if he was?"

Mrs Edwards ran a hand over her hair. "You know, I'm not sure that he would. He would probably have protected myself and the children from worry."

"Of course..." Yvonne nodded. "Thank you."

∽

"Kelly? Kelly?" Kate stretched out a hand in the semi-darkness. "Don't give up now..."

"I'm scared, Kate." The older woman's voice trembled and broke. "I know what happens next."

"No." The younger woman's voice was firm. "I won't let it."

"You can't stop it."

"There must be a way to get to him. He's got to have a weakness."

"I hit him once." Kelly sighed. "Hard... I cut his cheek."

"Well, there you go." Kate shifted position on the makeshift wooden bed, her shoulders hunched to avoid hitting her head on the planks above, on which Kelly lay. "How did you manage it?"

"He had let me off the chain, allowing me to wander around in here. I did everything he asked, and he started trusting me."

"God, that must have been hard... Being nice to him."

"It wasn't easy, believe me. But spitting and screaming at

him was getting me nowhere. I tried a different tack, and for a time, it worked. Then one day I thought I would escape, and I hit him with a heavy book he'd let me read. I was almost out of the hatch when he grabbed my legs."

"What did he do?"

"He beat me so badly, I thought I was going to die. I honestly thought he wouldn't stop. I didn't think I would survive that day, and I have not gone up against him since." Kelly rubbed her sunken eyes, her shoulders hunched. "If you ever attempt to leave, you'd better be damned sure you'll make it out of the hatch." She leaned forward, whispering down to Kate, over the side of her bed. "He's killed before."

"What?" Kate leaned back, wide-eyed. "You mean women like us?" She scanned the room, lit by a thread of tiny LED lights. A few books, a table and chairs, and their pathetic excuse for bunk beds with meagre throws. There was no hint that anyone else had ever been in their prison.

"I knew one of them." Kelly closed her eyes. "Her name was Nina. I never knew her surname. We only ever used our first names."

"Nina..." Kate repeated. "What happened? Are you telling me he murdered her?"

"I'm sure he did. He took her out of here one day and when he returned he was tetchy, shouting at me more than usual. I got the feeling she was no longer with us." Kelly shuddered.

"Maybe he let her go?" Kate asked, without conviction.

"Nina told me he killed another woman in front of her-"

"What?" Kate pulled at her chain, sitting upright on the edge of her bed.

"Nina said that the girl he strangled was called Mair, and that he had become bored with her."

"God..."

"It was after Nina didn't come back that I stopped all resistance. I hoped she'd escaped, but in my heart I knew she hadn't. He took her somewhere and ended her life." Kelly swallowed hard. "I'm sure of it, and I'm so scared he will do the same to us."

"Do you know how long you've been here?" Kate lay back, relaxing the pull of the shackle on her sore wrist.

"Not exactly, but I think there have been six winters since I was kidnapped, so it must be nearly seven years since I was abducted."

"Have you asked him the date?"

"He refuses to tell me. I can't orientate myself in time, except for the passing of winter, where the air from above is colder when he opens that hatch." She pulled a face. "You become sensitive to the slightest change. I don't think he heats the room up there."

"My last name is Hughes. I am Katherine Hughes, Kate for short."

"And I am Kelly Lewis. There are times, Katherine Hughes, I have wished you were not here, only because your presence makes it more likely he will get rid of me. But actually, I am so glad you are." She pressed her lips tight together and lay back.

"Are you okay?" Kate stared at the planks above.

"I'm frightened he's preparing to get rid of me. He keeps us for a few years, and then gets rid after bringing in someone new."

"And that someone is me."

"Yes."

"We will not let him hurt you, you hear me? Won't."

A door slammed, and something scraped the floor above them.

"Oh no, he's mad..." Kelly bit her lip. "Brace yourself."

They lay, dirt-smeared but defiant, stealing themselves for the abuse they were used to him inflicting on them, fighting back the nausea and gut-wrenching dread.

Kate clenched her fists. He could control her physical body, but not her mind. It didn't matter what he did, he would never have that.

16

SUSPICIOUS BEHAVIOURS

DC Callum Jones placed a pen behind his ear and leaned his chair back on two legs, cupping his hands together, lips pursed.

"Okay, what are you thinking?" Yvonne perched on the end of his desk. "What have you got for me?"

"Amir Khan..."

"What about him?" She rolled her sleeves up, head cocked.

"He was questioned back in two-thousand-seventeen in connection with the disappearance of Kelly Lewis. Apparently, he was the last known person to speak to her, having driven the taxi which took the girl and her bike to Welshpool. He was driving for Newtown Taxis. That was three years before he began working for himself."

"Really?" The DI leaned in. "What came from his interview? Did they clear him? Is he still a suspect?"

They had CCTV footage of the drop-off, and nothing to suggest he interacted with her afterwards. Although, crucially, there was nothing to confirm he didn't. There were no cameras along the waterway, and Khan had his lunch break not long after he dropped her off.

"Okay..." Yvonne nodded. "Callum, how long has Amir Khan been in the UK? Assuming the missing girl cases are related, could he have committed the earlier abductions?"

"That's why I find him so interesting... He arrived in Wales in two-thousand-five." The DC put his hands behind his head. "So, he has the potential to be our guy."

"You could be right. We have a connection to the disappearances of both Kate Hughes and Kelly lewis. If he was the abductor, it would explain why he would be reluctant to use his taxi a second time and use a van instead."

"Right..." Callum swung his chair back onto all four legs. "That's what I'm thinking."

"We'll get a warrant to search Amir Khan's place. For all we know, his lodgers may have unwittingly supplied him with a knowledge of Kate Hughes's routine."

∼

The Newtown Garvey-and-Griffiths store was the calmest she had seen it. Staff milled around, or else checked the shelves they had already checked ten minutes before.

The DI waited on a chair at the back of the warehouse, next to the office door, staring at piles of seasoned timber. She checked her watch, confirming it had been five minutes since she had last checked it. Don Akeman was late.

"Would you like a cup of tea while you wait?" Simon Jones grimaced. "I'm sorry he's not back yet. He should have returned by now. We can put the kettle on, but can't access the office. Don took the keys with him." He shrugged. "I tried ringing his mobile, but I don't think he has a signal."

"It's all right." She raised a hand. "I'm fine, I can wait. But a cuppa would be lovely, thank you."

"Oh..." He stopped in his tracks. "I can't believe I've been that stupid." He raised both hands to his head.

"The kettle is in the office?" She grinned.

He nodded. "Bugger... I'm sorry."

"It's all right, honestly. I'm good. Don't let me interrupt your work."

He took a step away from her, then turned back. "Do you know any more about Mal's death? Have you any idea who killed him?" He pushed his hands deep into the pockets of his workshop coat.

"Nothing I can tell you, I'm afraid." She scoured his face. "Have you had any thoughts?"

Somewhere on the shop floor, a metal implement clanged onto the concrete floor.

She put a hand to her chest, her breathing sped up.

"Sorry..." He pulled a face. "Sounds like someone dropped something. I'm used to it."

"Can I ask you something, Simon?"

"Sure." He shifted the weight between his feet.

"When Garvey-and-Griffiths had three stores, and someone won the staff bonus, did the whole store benefit?"

He nodded. "The rest of the staff would have their Christmas meals paid for at a restaurant."

This confirmed what Rhiannon had told her. "Were there other benefits?"

"Not unless you count having your mugshot in the local rag." He grimaced. "I'm not that photogenic."

"Was Mal Edwards competitive?"

He shook his head. "I think I told you before, Mal helped people out of kindness. I don't think he did it for the bonuses."

Another clatter rang out somewhere in the middle of the aisles.

"Look, I'd better get on. I'm sure Don won't be long." Jones turned on his heel, striding between the aisles in the noise's direction.

Yvonne checked her watch, wondering whether she ought to return another time.

"Sorry, Inspector..." A red-faced Don Akeman approached from her left. "Personal problems... I took the office keys with me by mistake. They were in my overalls pocket. I don't normally take them with me. Come in, please."

He unlocked the door, wiping perspiration from his forehead with a hanky. "It's warming up out there," he said, motioning her inside. "Please sit down. I'll make a brew."

She had not asked Simon if he was upset whenever Mal won the staff bonus, because he was the only staff member there, and she hadn't wanted to interfere with the running of the store. Now the manager was back. She was ready to confront them with Rhiannon Edwards' perspective.

"There you go." Akeman handed her a mug of tea. "And I am sorry you had to wait so long."

"You're probably wondering why I wanted to speak with you again?" She eyed him as he sat.

He met her gaze. "I'm assuming it's about Mal, and nothing to do with my charm and good looks?" He grinned, but his face straightened when she didn't respond. He cleared his throat. "I was wondering, yes."

"I've been told you were disappointed when Mal kept winning the staff bonus."

"Maybe a little. I kept hoping I might get it. But to be honest, I always knew I wouldn't. I could never find the time to do all the extra-curricular stuff that Mal did. The man was phenomenal. I don't know where he got his energy from. It was as much as I could do to drag myself home after a busy day here. Mal would often go off to see a customer after work. I mean, who does that? So yeah, I would have liked the big bonus, but I never really expected to get it. If I'd wanted it that badly, I'd have put in the extra effort." He stared at her, rubbing his chin. "I wouldn't have killed Mal. I would simply have done extra for the clients."

The DI nodded. "Have you remembered any more about that time? Anything about Mal, and what was happening in his life? I know it was a long time ago, but-"

"There was something…" He frowned in concentration.

"Go on…"

"The day before he went missing, Mal popped out in the early afternoon to see a client project. When he returned, he looked out of sorts."

Yvonne sat upright. "What do you mean, out of sorts?"

"He seemed flustered. Twice, he approached me as though he wanted to say something, but he didn't speak."

"Did you ask him if he was all right?"

"I think I did. I can't really recall. He didn't give me an explanation. I was busy on the shop floor. The manager was off sick, and I was the only staff member here for a couple of hours while Mal was out. When you work in a builder's merchants, you find that most of the customers need advice and practical know-how. It can be pretty intense."

"Can you remember how Mal was the following morning? The day he disappeared?"

"He seemed fine, but I might not have noticed if he wasn't. It had been another hectic start to the day, and I left Simon and Mal to it. Mal probably went to get some air with his sandwiches, I thought, and I didn't blame him."

"Do you know which client he had been to see on the day he came back out of sorts?"

"No, he didn't say and, back then, we didn't have a lone-working policy. We keep a log these days, so in the rare event we go out to advise on a project, or if we are doing a delivery, we fill in the name and address of the customer if it isn't already known. Other staff members always know where we are."

"I see." She checked her watch. "I was hoping to speak to Simon, but I've run out of time. Could you ask him to call me when it's convenient?"

"Yes, of course." Akeman rose from his seat. "I'll ask him on his next break."

"Thanks." She headed for the door. "If you find out who Mal went to see, please let me know."

"I will."

17

THE RAID

"Come in." DCI Llewelyn sounded rough.

"Sorry to bother you, sir. I wanted to discuss the Mal Edwards case with you."

He was swimming in paper, his hair mussed, and sleeves rolled up.

"Is now a good time?" she asked, wondering how he made sense of the chaos on his desk.

He sighed, running a hand through his ragged hair. "Now is as good a time as any. I've got a meeting with the chief in half-an-hour, and I wanted to ask you about progress on your cases."

"We're still looking for a motive for Mal's murder. One angle we're examining involves his work clients. Maybe one of them did it, but he was well-liked by them, so I'm not hopeful of finding answers in that direction. I am wondering if he was merely in the wrong place at the wrong time, when he wandered up the lane from work with his sandwiches."

"If it was a stranger-murder, you've got your work cut out... What did you want to ask me?"

"Can we widen the search in the fields where Mal's remains were found?"

He frowned. "Why?"

"We may have a serial killer in the area and, if we do, there may be others buried in that field."

"You're asking for a lot of resource, time and manpower."

"I know."

"And it's not something we can use volunteers for..."

"Will you speak to the chief? We haven't found the weapon used to kill Mal. It could be up there."

"I can ask him, but have you got anything else I can give him in the meantime?" He placed both hands on his hips.

"A former colleague thinks Mal was agitated after visiting one of their customers at home."

"Did the colleague know why?"

"No, but I'm speaking to another of Mal's former colleagues today, and I will ask him about it."

"Fine." Llewelyn sighed. "What about Kate Hughes? Are there any clues as to her whereabouts?"

She shook her head. "We're looking into a taxi driver whose vehicle was seen close to the location she is believed to have gone missing, near where her bike was found in the canal. I'm not ready to update you yet, sir. I'll get the file together, and leave it on your desk tomorrow, if that is okay? The cab driver's house will be searched, and I'll need a warrant. We should have that by tomorrow morning. In the meantime, we have all units keeping an eye out for Kate, and posters all over social media."

"Good, all keep me updated."

"Yes, sir."

∼

AMIR KHAN OWNED a white Georgian town house with black-glossed windows, a front door accessed via an old carriage arch, and a cobbled passageway which led to a tiny yard. The latter was traversed by lines of washing drying in the breeze.

Yvonne followed the search team, waiting outside until they had served the warrant, and explained the reason for the raid.

When she entered, several uniformed officers were already sifting through belongings in nylon gloves while Khan protested for several minutes until giving up, hands on hips.

"Amir..." she approached as he scowled at the other officers. "Do you have a basement?"

"Yes, why? Do you think I have girls stashed down there? You know how ridiculous that is? I can hardly afford to feed myself, let alone a harem of girls."

"Is it down there?" She pointed to a small door at the back of the hallway.

"Yes."

"Is it locked?"

"The key is in that drawer." He pointed to a wooden bureau behind her.

Yvonne opened it, finding a small bunch of keys. "Which is the one for the basement?" she asked, fanning them out for him to show her the right one.

"Don't go in too fast, you'll scare them," he mocked.

She strode through the hallway to the door at the end. The lock was stiff, but she forced it open, feeling around in the dark for a light switch.

"There's no bulb down there," Khan shouted.

She had discovered that for herself. She resisted the urge

to swear. "Can I borrow your torch?" she asked of the nearest constable.

He passed it to her before going into the lounge, where another officer was questioning Reza Hassani.

The DI turned her attention to the uneven stone steps leading down into the old wine cellar, scraping off the cobwebs which clung to her and spitting out the one which hit her in the face.

No-one had been down there in a while. On the floor lay the dusty remnants of coal, a pile of broken wooden chairs, and an old blanket chest with a damaged clasp. The latter was empty.

Aside from that, a pair of faded yellow curtains lay in a heap alongside the head of an iron bedstead.

"It's clear down here," she announced, disappointed at not finding Kate Hughes, but relieved at the absence of a body. If Amir Khan was holding Kate captive, it wasn't in the basement of his house.

They went through every drawer of every cupboard, the wardrobes, and cabinets. There was nothing out of the ordinary.

∽

IT WAS A DEFLATED Yvonne who went home that evening, her mind clouded and body stiff.

Even the lights streaming from the windows of her home failed to lift her spirits.

She opened the front door to soft strains of jazz.

"You made it home, then?" Tasha grinned, meeting her in the hallway. The smile faded when she saw Yvonne's tired face. She put a hand on her partner's shoulder, her forehead creased with concern. "Are you okay?"

The DI forced a smile. "I will be. It's been one of those days." She kicked her shoes off in the hall before following the psychologist through to the lounge, where a birch wood fire burned in the hearth.

"You look worn out." Tasha took her coat. "Get yourself warmed up. I've got chicken casserole in the oven."

Yvonne sank into the cushions on the sofa, thinking of Kate Hughes and Mal Edwards. "We're no further forward," she said aloud. "Every time I think we are getting somewhere, we hit the wall."

"Want to talk about it?" The psychologist joined her on the couch, dressed in a loose tee-shirt and lounge pants.

"I don't want to put it on you, Tasha. You have enough on your plate with your London case. And, as for profiling, I'm not really sure what we are looking at. We have a seventeen-year-old cold case involving the murder of a middle-aged man, and a missing teenager whose disappearance may or may not be linked to the disappearances of at least two other young women stretching back to two-thousand-five."

"Tell me about your cold case. Who was he, and what happened?" The psychologist handed her a glass of chardonnay from the coffee table. "Sip this, dinner won't be long."

Yvonne accepted the glass. "I can tell you what we know. Unfortunately, it won't take long."

She related Mal's circumstances, disappearance, and death to Tasha, explaining how the remains were found, and the lack of credible motives. "It makes me wonder whether we are looking at a serial killer. Maybe Mal was simply in the wrong place at the wrong time."

Tasha frowned. "And there was no change in his behaviour leading up to the disappearance?"

"Not really..." Yvonne took another sip of wine. "Except,

a former colleague said Mal appeared agitated after visiting a customer project in the days prior to vanishing."

"Do you know anything about the project? Or the customer?"

The DI shook her head. "The colleague can't remember, but I have Mal's notebook. It has the names and addresses of some of his clients, and plans and sketches he drew, which are presumably outlines for their proposed builds. And that's the problem... Mal had a unique way of doing things. Although he has the details of the clients, he hasn't associated the sketches with the individuals. We're left guessing which plans go with which customer."

"Oh..."

"I have his notebook in my bag, if you'd like to see it?"

Tasha nodded. "I would."

Yvonne retrieved her bag from the hallway. "I think this book was more of an aide-mémoire for Mal. He was the only one who was supposed to see it. It's probably why he didn't have more organised notes. It was his ideas doodling pad."

"Don't they have an official record of the projects archived somewhere?"

"No, they don't. Garvey-and-Griffiths are a builder's merchant. They stock tools and materials. Mal gave customers practical advice and guidance in his spare time. Out of the goodness of his heart, I'm told. There was an added incentive for him as a works Christmas bonus, if he drummed up the most business and provided the best customer experience. There were three stores and around twenty total staff members."

"How much was the bonus worth?"

"Two thousand pounds."

"That's not enough motive for a murder."

"I don't think so either, which is why I have all but discounted the bonus as a reason."

"So then, we come back to the projects. You said Mal was agitated after viewing one."

"I did, although I only have the word of one of his former colleagues, so it isn't set in stone."

"Okay..." Tasha nodded. "May I?" She reached for the notebook.

Yvonne watched her partner's forehead furrow while leafing through it. "It's a little chaotic, isn't it?"

"Like you said, it seems to be more of an aid to his memory than anything else."

The DI moved closer to examine the pages with her partner. "We were wondering what this could have been." She tapped her finger on the schematic of the mystery room. "We think it could be a sort of underground bomb shelter."

Tasha frowned. "It could be... There are beds, built-in storage, and air vents. I guess active air vents would be needed if it's underground. There's other stuff drawn in it which isn't labelled."

"Mal wasn't in the habit of explaining everything in his drawings, unfortunately. We have to guess what he's depicting."

The psychologist scratched her head. "I don't think this is an air-raid shelter, though."

"No?"

"Look at the door. It opens outwards from the top of the build as you would expect but, if that is the opening mechanism, it's on the outside."

"Okay..."

"How would you get out? You might be safe from all the

bombing, but you're going to starve because the door handle is on the outside."

"Oh my God... You're right. I didn't notice that. How could it be a bomb shelter if the people inside couldn't open the hatch? Well-spotted, Tasha."

"The sirens blare. The owner and his family head through the hatch and down the ladder, into their brand new vented shelter, but they can't close the door properly and, if they do, they're stuck."

"I can't believe I missed that. Someone could come along and bolt them in. There would be no escape."

"That is no air raid shelter. It could be some sort of cold storage bunker?"

"Except, when have you ever had a cold room with bunk beds?"

They looked at each other. "Are you thinking what I'm thinking?" Tasha asked.

"This could be a prison... like that Fritz guy who kept his daughter trapped in a purpose-built room all those years."

"Perhaps your murder victim realised what his client was building and confronted him?"

"He may have ruminated after talking to the customer and drawing the sketch. Maybe that was why he was agitated."

"Right, and if the owner of this bunker killed Mal, he wasn't intending to use it to store food."

Yvonne nodded. "Well, it's something to work with. I can't substantiate any of this until I find out who the customer was. But thank you, Tasha, you have helped me see a way forward. I'll speak with Mal's last known clients again. This time, I'll be more specific about my questioning."

18

ON THE RUN

"Ahmed Syeed has gone on the run," Dewi announced.

"What? Why?" Yvonne was surprised to see her DS in the office before her.

"Your guess is as good as mine. According to Reza Hassani, Ahmed was walking home with him when he saw the raid at the house, and took off. Left in the clothes he was wearing, with a small backpack and the money in his pocket, which wouldn't have been much. We've put out an alert, but he hasn't been picked up yet."

"Did he think it was an immigration raid?" She tossed her suede jacket onto the back of her chair.

"I would say that's fairly likely unless he has something to hide, such as the whereabouts of Kate Hughes."

"If he's picked up, let me know."

"There's something else, Yvonne."

"Yes?"

"I've been looking into the possibility that Mal Edwards was killed elsewhere, and transported to the field above Garthowen."

"Go on..."

"Those hills have several off-road vehicle trails open to the public. They are well known only to the members of off-roading clubs. However, you can look them up online easily enough. There is a trail that runs close to where Mal's remains were found. Within metres, in fact."

"So his body could have been transported and buried there, rather than Mal be lured up there alive?"

"Right."

"Maybe he didn't walk up the fields at all. Perhaps he had a meeting with someone somewhere else, and something happened."

Yvonne told him about the conversation with Tasha the evening before, and the contentious bunker.

"It's a solid angle to explore, and probably more of a motive for murder than the Christmas bonus. But what are we saying here? That one of his customers wanted a bunker to keep someone else captive?"

"Why not? We know it happens. It may be rare, but such monsters exist. I intend to question Mal's last known clients again." Her eyes glistened with determination. "I suspect that's where the answer lies. In the meantime, Dewi, could you chase up the whereabouts of Ahmed Syeed? If he is on the run because he knows something about Kate Hughes, the sooner we find him, the better. The DCI is after me for answers."

"Right you are, ma'am. Leave it to me, but you might have to make your own brew."

∼

"Ah, Yvonne..." DCI Llewelyn approached her desk. "We've had the go-ahead from the chief to widen the search of the fields above Garthowen, but we've to keep ground disruption to a minimum. He's approved the funds for a geophysics survey. They can map the area, and we can concentrate on any anomalies they find."

"That's great, thank you, sir."

"Do you have an interim report for me?"

She grimaced.

"You said you'd have it ready for me this morning?"

"I know, and I'm almost ready. We have several irons in the fire right now, and I need to get on with it. I can update you later, I promise."

"You'd better, Giles." He grinned. "And it had better be good."

∽

"Callum?" She approached the DC as he scoured CCTV footage.

"Ma'am?" He paused the video, leaning back in his chair.

"I can see you're busy, but I am going to see some of Mal Edwards' old clients. Can I ask you a favour?"

"Fire away." He nodded.

"Can you find out when David Cadman and Bryn Ellis moved into their current homes? And could you ask Dai to find out who is living in their old properties, and whether they have found any hidden rooms or tunnels, either below their houses, or dug under the garden?"

"Like a cellar?"

"Or a bunker."

"Will do... What are you thinking?"

"Dewi will fill you in. I've got to go. I'm still working it all out."

"Wait, should you be going to see them on your own?" Callum raised a brow. "The DCI better not find out."

"I have my spray, and an alarm, and Dewi knows where I am going. I'm off to speak with Wyn Thomas, Bryn Ellis, and David Cadman again, and should be back late afternoon. After each address, I'll text you to let you know I am okay."

"Got it."

"Don't forget to find out the information regarding Ellis' and Cadman's old addresses."

"I won't." He lifted his hand to his temple in mock salute.

Yvonne laughed. "Don't be cheeky."

19

THE MISSING SHELTER

Wyn Thomas was the only one of Mal's final three clients who had not moved home in the intervening years, having inherited the family farm from his father. Yvonne thought it best to begin with him.

She texted Dewi to tell him she had arrived at Erw Las before donning boots from the back of the car to traverse the muddy yard.

"Over here..." Wyn's voice emanated from the cowshed.

She entered the building, but couldn't see him while her eyes recovered from the bright sunshine outside.

"Here," he called.

She found him, pitchfork in hand, mucking out in muddy overalls and wellingtons. "Do you still have a few minutes, Wyn?"

"Sure..." He put his fork down. "What can I do for you?" He pushed the tweed flat cap back off his forehead.

"Do you have cold storage on the farm?"

"Cold storage?" He frowned. "Yes, we have a cold room for the cheeses. Is that what you mean?"

"Could I see it?" She tried to appear relaxed, though her stomach churned.

He shrugged. "Sure, I don't see why not. We keep the room fairly sterile, though-"

"I don't think I'll need to go inside. Simply look, if that is all right?"

"Fine, whatever..." He led her across the yard to an extension at the back of the house. "It's in here."

"Okay."

He punched numbers into an electronic keypad, and a loud click signalled the unlocking of the door. Wyn pulled a heavy duty handle towards him, and a rush of chilled air washed over her, accompanied by the hum of a generator.

"This is where we store our butter and cheeses. We supply local shops and farmer's markets from here." He stepped aside, allowing her to see the rows of metal shelves stacked with round cheeses and wrapped butter blocks.

"Thank you, Wyn." She stepped away as he shut the door, the outside air supplying a cushion of warmth. She was satisfied the cold room was exactly as he described. "Do you have other storage facilities?"

"We have barns, if that is what you mean?"

"What about underground?"

"Not unless you include the slurry pit." He grinned. "I really don't think you'll want to go down there."

"Did Mal help you design any of these rooms?"

He shook his head. "No, he didn't. The cold room for our dairy produce was installed by the company who makes them. It was adapted from our old pantry. Mal had nothing to do with that."

"And the slurry pit?"

"The slurry pit is over a hundred years old, I believe. I remember it being here when I was a small child. It wasn't covered by a grill in those days. It wasn't unheard of for kids to fall in and drown. Not in ours, like. But it happened. Mal wasn't born when that was installed."

"And you have no other underground pits or rooms?"

"No... Why do you ask, anyway?"

"We're trying to put a timeline together for Mal's last few weeks. We know he had a few projects on the go, and we're making a list."

"I'm sorry that I couldn't be of more help."

"Do you have a cellar?"

"Yes, we store root vegetables in it, along with wine and meat. You're welcome to see it."

She glanced at her watch. "That's all right, Wyn. I don't need to see your cellar, unless Mal had a hand in redesigning it?"

He shook his head. "It hasn't been changed for hundreds of years."

She pulled her coat tight around her. "Thank you for your time. I'll be on my way."

"Take care, Inspector," he said, turning back to his cowshed.

∼

NEXT ON HER list was Bryn Ellis, the artist who ran a business from his home in Aberhafesp and who, during Mal's time, had lived on the Milford Road in Newtown.

The DI had phoned ahead to warn of her visit and was surprised by Bryn's response when he opened the door.

He stared at her, wide-eyed and open-mouthed.

"Are you okay? I telephoned your wife to say I was coming?" She raised her brows.

"Elyn had to go out. She left me a note, but I forgot to

look at it. She rarely disturbs me when I have the office door shut." He rubbed his forehead. "You gave me a shock... I wasn't expecting anyone. I thought maybe Elyn had an accident, and you were here to give me bad news."

"Oh no, it's nothing like that." She studied his face. "I came to talk with you again about your interactions with Malcolm Edwards."

He took a step back. "You'd better come in then, but I don't have long, I'm afraid." He led her through to the lounge, looking more relaxed than he sounded in cut-off jeans and a tee-shirt, his feet bare.

Copious sunlight flooded the bay window. "I've just boiled the kettle. Do you take milk and sugar?"

"Milk, no sugar, please." She sat on the cloth sofa, its two-tone grey matched the shag-pile rug in front of the fireplace, and the austerity of the modern art on the walls.

"I'm sorry about the confusion," he said, returning with a large tray on which clattered a teapot, cups, and saucers. "My wife went into town. She'll be back in about an hour."

"That's all right. It was you I came to see."

"I've cut some fruitcake," he said, seeming not to hear her. "Elyn baked it yesterday." He gave her a wink. "It's the best cake in Newtown."

Yvonne had been about to turn down the cake, but felt she couldn't after that. She accepted the tea and side plate with good grace.

"To what do I owe this surprise visit?" He was silhouetted in an armchair by the window, making it difficult for her to see his expressions.

She had to squint to see him. Either he was insensitive, or this was a deliberate choice.

Either way, he gave no acknowledgement of her discomfort, sipping his tea and munching cake.

Somewhere in the corner, a clock ticked.

The DI cleared her throat. "When did you move here from Milford Road, Bryn?"

He looked up at the ceiling. "When did I move here? Wow, er... it would have to be about thirteen or fourteen years ago. Let's see, I started the business ten years ago, and the move was a few years before that. Two-thousand-eight is the year I have in my head. I'm fairly sure it was the summer of that year."

"Did you alter the last house in any way? Maybe adding a cellar or more storage?"

He raised a brow. "No."

"What about a bomb shelter?"

"A bomb shelter? No," he snorted. "Mind you, the way things are going with Russia, I wonder whether maybe we ought to have one. But we have never had such a thing. Why did you ask that?"

"We are trying to make sense of some sketches Mal did. One of them looked like it might be a plan of a shelter. I thought perhaps he had drawn it for a customer, but of course, he could have drawn it for himself." This wasn't exactly true but, if Bryn Ellis was up to no good, she didn't want him destroying evidence.

"I see what you're saying." He rubbed his chin, looking at the floor.

"Do you know anyone in the area who has such a thing?"

"I don't, I'm sorry. I haven't heard of anyone having a nuclear shelter since the eighties. Mal must have known someone who wanted one, I guess... But that person wasn't me or anyone I know. I wish I could help you, but I can't."

The rest of her meeting with Ellis was awkward, as he

had little else to say, and she had a struggle to finish the fruitcake.

As she left Aberhafesp, Yvonne couldn't help feeling unsure about him. The folded arms, and sitting with the sun at his back. It felt to her like he had needed to control the exchange.

Her mobile vibrated in her pocket. "Dewi?"

"I'm checking you're all right. We hadn't heard from you in a while."

"Oh, I'm sorry... I'm fine. I've got one more visit to see David Cadman in Llanfyllin, and I'll be on my way back. I'll ring you in around an hour, when I've finished with him, okay?"

"Right you are. Don't forget..."

She laughed. "I won't. Get back on the job... I shall want an update later."

∾

∾

DAVID CADMAN WAS on his knees in the garden, holding a trowel in one gloved hand, and weeds in the other. His knees clicked as he stood. "Inspector Giles?" He threw the plant debris into a rusty wheel barrow and peeled off the gardening gloves. "I had thought you wouldn't get here. I got on with a few bits while I waited." He brushed the front of his trousers with his hands. "I'm glad you made it. I need a break."

"I'm sorry I'm late, Mister Cadman."

He led her to the round wooden table. "It's no problem. I had nowhere else to be. "

"Were you married?" If she wasn't a police officer, this

might have been insensitive, but she was curious that she had neither seen nor heard of a partner.

"Are you propositioning me, Inspector?"

"No." Her gaze did not waver.

He cleared his throat. "I have never been married. I lived with a woman called Marianne for twelve years. We split up when I was thirty-eight. I have been single ever since. I've dated, but nothing serious."

"Are you comfortable here? It's a big place to occupy alone. How many bedrooms do you have?"

"Three. It would have been four, but I converted one of them to a study. I like the space, and I really don't mind rolling around here on my own."

"You have a lovely garden." She cast her eyes around the lawn, trees, and shrubs. "It's immaculate."

"Thank you." He grinned. "It keeps me out of mischief."

Her gaze wandered to the concrete cube that he used as a workshop. "What's down there?" Yvonne referred to the end of the garden, where it narrowed to a point which was all but hidden by a thick conifer hedge. "Is that the roof of a shed I can see?"

"It's my old shed, yes. I don't use it much anymore." He turned towards the house.

"May I see it?"

He raised both eyebrows. "If you really want to?"

"I do."

"Wait here, I'll get the key." He looked like he wanted to say something more, but thought better of it, striding toward the house.

She wandered the lawn, ambling towards the conifer hedge past two apple trees.

"The keys."

She jumped.

Cadman had come up behind her without making a sound. "It's padlocked," he explained, before leading her through a narrow gate in the hedge. "The grass is a little overgrown here. I have given it over to the wildlife. I have a few tools that store in the shed but, aside from that, it's for the insects and animals. Most of the tools I need on a day-to-day basis are kept in the cube." He unlocked the door and stepped back, allowing her inside of the structure ahead of him.

She swallowed hard, holding the mace spray in her right coat pocket. "You're very organised." She eyed the tins of paint on the shelving. All labels faced forward.

To her right, a folded portable workbench leaned against the wall. The only other furniture inside was a wooden farmhouse chair. The flooring comprised grass matting. She rubbed it with the toe of her shoe.

"I have the flooring to protect the old wood underneath. I used to do a lot more work in here before the cube was finished."

She lifted her eyes from the matting to his.

"You want to see what is underneath?" He delivered the question like he'd read her mind. Any hint of a smile was gone.

She wiped her forehead with a hanky as he carried out first the chair, then the workbench.

Finally, he lifted the edge of the matting, peeling it back to reveal the floor of the shed.

She looked for any sign of a doorway or removable planks. There was nothing obvious.

"Happy?" A mocking smile curled his upper lip. It seemed contemptuous.

"Perfectly." Something about him put her out of sorts. Her fingers tightened on the mace.

"Is that everything, Inspector? Only, I've got to get on with the weeding. If I leave it any later this year, the roots will be too deep, and I'll never get rid of them."

"Yes, I should get back." She thought of giving some trite explanation for her visit, but it was clear from his half-lidded look he knew he was on the suspect list. The hands behind his back and jutting chin told her he didn't care.

20

A DREADFUL FATE

The hatch creaked open. Dust swirled in the cold musty air pouring in.

Kelly had moved closer to Kate, her chain stretched far enough to sit on the lower bunk with her fellow captive.

As he entered, Kate felt her friend shake, and smelled the dank, sweat-soaked odour of dread. She watched him closely, assessing his mood. Were they safe or not? It was no way to live, but she was getting used to it.

He came down the ladder, silent, catlike. He was dangerous like this. It meant he was planning something. The wrong word could bring a devastating outburst. A thrown chair, a pate of food up the wall, a slap or a punch.

Both girls were silent.

"I'm taking you for a ride in a couple of days, Kelly. I thought you might enjoy a change of scenery." He took small bottles from a backpack, placing them on the floor along with a foil-wrapped stack of sandwiches.

Kelly and Kate exchanged glances, knowing nothing

good would come of her accompanying him out of their hole.

The older woman's voice shook. "I'm good, actually. I really don't need to go anywhere."

"I thought you'd be desperate to get out of here." He shot her a narrow-eyed look.

She was, but not in the way he intended. "I'm not well." She held her stomach, bending over. Feigning illness wasn't hard. She had lost a considerable amount of muscle mass during her time in captivity. Parts of her were always hurting.

"The fresh air will do you good."

"I'll come, too." Kate didn't want to leave her friend alone with him.

"Two's company," he growled. "You'll stay where you are. I have other plans for you."

Kate swallowed hard. She thought of striking him, bringing something down on his head with all of her might. But this might only make him mad. She didn't want to make things worse for Kelly.

~

THE ROOM BUZZED with bodies rushing back and forth, phone calls being made and received, the hammering of keyboards, and conversations happening on the fly.

Today was the day geo-forensics would start their survey of the Garthowen fields where Malcolm Edwards' remains had been buried.

The team was split in two, with Dai and Callum on the Kate Hughes investigation, and Yvonne and Dewi on the cold case. Uniformed officers were present for the briefing on their roles in each investigation.

Dewi strode up to Yvonne as she pored over maps of the area to be surveyed. "The geophysics guys are on site, Yvonne. The weather should hold, and they are good to go."

She looked through the window at the overcast sky and nodded. "Let's hope it doesn't rain. What about the dogs?" she asked, referring to the specially trained cadaver-detecting canines they were hoping to borrow from Wrexham. Able to detect the scent of remains for decades even after burial, they would help narrow the search area for the geophysics team, if they could get them.

He shook his head. "We may not be in luck. They're being used over the border." He pushed his hands deep into his pockets. "Geophysics want to know how wide they should survey."

The DI pursed her lips. "I think we should stick to the field where Mal's remains were. If we're right, and the killer drove his body up there using the four-by-four trails, he's likely to have done the same with any other bodies. Unfortunately, we have a delicate balance between resource and the likelihood of finding anything. Everything we do has got to be cost-effective and proportionate. So we stick with that field for now and, if we do eventually get the dogs, we can cast a wider net using them."

"Makes sense." Dewi nodded. "Oh, The County Times and several other newspapers have been in touch. So has Welsh Television News. They're sending people up there."

She sighed. "Okay, but make sure they know to stay outside of the cordon. Have a word with Inspector Davies," she said, referring to the uniformed inspector in charge of the officers securing the scene. "Ask him to ensure they keep any onlookers back. The last thing we need is a chaotic scene." She smoothed down her skirt and pushed stray hair from her face. "Callum said a psychic telephoned yesterday, saying she'd had visions of more bodies by a hedge and a large puddle."

Dewi pulled a face.

She grinned. "Exactly... It's likely we'll have a lot more than just newspapers and television journalists to deal with."

"Righty-oh." Dewi took his hands out of his pockets. "I'll get onto Davies now, make sure he's prepared. As soon as our excavation is reported anywhere, we'll likely have an exodus out there."

"Mal's wife is aware." Yvonne nodded. "She doesn't want to visit the field, but we should keep her informed. If anyone else, such as a former colleague of Mal's, turns up? I'd be interested to know who. Our killer will probably watch."

"I'll make sure we get names and addresses."

She turned back to her map, something tugging at the back of her mind, a feeling she couldn't quite bring to the surface. She gave herself a mental shake. There was work to be done.

~

It was mid-afternoon when the call came through to say they had found something.

The DI and Dewi drove up to Garthowen to see for themselves, parking at the top of the estate, and entering the fields via a style, past an already sizeable gathering.

She flashed her badge at a young PC as he approached to enquire who they were.

He nodded and stepped aside.

Several news teams had taken up position outside of the cordon, eager to find out what was going on.

Two reporters approached them, one with a microphone

which he pushed into Yvonne's face. He had an Irish accent. "Am I right in thinking you're the lead investigator, DI Yvonne Giles?"

"I'm sorry," she pushed the microphone away. "I can't talk right now. There will be a press conference later."

"Move back," Dewi ordered, waving his hands to reinforce the message.

"Are there more bodies up there?" The journalist persisted.

"We don't know," she answered truthfully. A geophysical anomaly was not necessarily a shallow grave.

"But you believe there are?"

This time, she didn't answer, heading under the cordon and towards a large tent over to their left.

Inside, a blonde-haired male of around thirty-five, in jeans and a blue shirt, was bent over a laptop screen, rubbing his chin.

"DI Yvonne Giles, and DS Dewi Hughes," she announced.

"Andrew Riley." He shook her hand. "Myself and Steven Jenkins are from the geo-forensics team. I've got the easy bit..." He pointed at his screen. "Steven is out there doing the legwork, the conductivity survey. It feeds the results through to me in here." He smiled. "If it rains, I'm the one who stays dry."

"What are we looking at?" she asked, approaching his screen.

Dewi cleared his throat. "Er... I'll be outside, Yvonne. I'll see who we've got up here."

She waved, turning her attention back to Riley and his laptop.

He tapped the screen twice, and an image opened, revealing three roughly oblong shapes at varying angles to each other. "We have a cluster of major anomalies, which include the shallow grave found previously. As you can see..." He pointed at the screen. "There are two further ground disturbances of a similar size and shape to the first. Looking at them, I'd say we have two more graves here. Three, if you include the original. Steven still has ground to cover, so we'll finish that before I show you our conclusions."

She studied the screen. "It certainly looks like we have another two graves." She pursed her lips. "It looks like we have ourselves a serial killer."

He nodded. "It looks that way. We've informed Scenes of Crime, and there's a team on their way. I believe your pathologist is also heading over. If they get here soon, they could complete the excavation before dark."

She nodded. "This is excellent work, thank you."

"No problem..." His eyes twinkled. "It's nice to get out somewhere different."

The DI left the tent, traversing soft mud, glad of her boots, to peer at Riley's colleague as he painstakingly moved his conductivity meter step-by-step over the turf. He didn't look up, remaining engrossed in his work. Over to her right, numbered markers were surrounded by a mini-cordon showing the positions of the suspected graves, mere metres from where Mal Edwards had been found.

Dewi approached her from behind. "The psychic arrived."

"Sorry?" She turned to where he stood, catching his breath.

"The psychic... She's over there." He pointed to the crowd gathering behind the main cordon. "See the middle-aged lady in bohemian dress, with purple hair? Her name is Penny." He smothered a grin.

"What's the matter?" She raised an eyebrow. "Haven't you seen purple hair before?"

"It's not that..." He reddened in the face, snorting to control laughter.

"Then what?" She asked, frowning.

He cleared his throat. "Her name is Penny Farthing."

"Penny Farthing? Are you having me on, Dewi Hughes?"

"No."

"Are you yanking my chain?"

"No, seriously... She told me with a straight face that her name is Penny Farthing."

"Her parents had a sense of humour." Yvonne grinned. "I like her already."

"She said she knows there are bodies by a hedge with a large puddle."

"Well, in this terrain and with this weather, that would be a good bet. But she's only partially right. There are at least two more anomalies, probably graves, around fifteen feet from the hedge. There isn't a puddle in sight. But don't disappoint her now... She'll find out soon enough."

"Right you are, ma'am."

"SOCO and Hanson are on their way, Dewi. We will know if they are graves in the next hour or two."

"Right, I thought I'd check out the rest of the crowd over there. Find out who is showing an interest, and whether it is healthy or unhealthy."

"Good... Make sure uniform is logging everyone, will you? I want names and addresses."

"Will do."

As she scanned the growing crowd, Yvonne spotted Simon Jones, Mal's former colleague, towering above the others.

He caught sight of her walking towards him and melted back into the crowd.

By the time she arrived at the cordon, he was gone. There was no sign of him anywhere.

"Dewi? Did you see Simon Jones?" she called to her sergeant.

"No, I didn't. Is he here?"

Yvonne frowned. "He was, but now he's gone." She checked her watch. It was mid-afternoon. Jones ought to be at work.

She was still pondering this, and hadn't seen Penny Farthing approach from the other side of the cordon.

"You're the police officer, aren't you? You're the lead investigator?"

"I'm Yvonne Giles, yes." She took a step towards the psychic. "Can I help you?"

"I saw you..." Penny narrowed her eyes, leaning her head at an angle and swaying. "I knew it was you I saw by the graves."

"Which graves?"

"The graves of those girls... You were there. I saw you in my dream. They were screaming... those graves. Two girls. You were there."

"I'm sorry, Ms Farthing, I don't know what you mean. Are you telling me you think there are females buried here?"

"Yes, young women... Two or three, I can't be sure."

"And how would you know that?" Yvonne cocked her head, taking in the other woman's spaced-out demeanour, and huge hoop earrings that flopped around every time she spoke. The air around had a strong smell of incense.

"I saw it, I told you. They screamed in my dreams. I saw you, too."

"I was in your dreams?"

"Yes... standing by the graves. Standing in water."

The DI shuddered despite herself. "And how did you know it was me?"

"I saw your face."

Yvonne had been in the local newspapers before. It wasn't surprising that she would appear as the police officer in Penny's dreams. She said so.

"Oh no, Inspector, I had never seen you before. Only in my dreams." She took hold of Yvonne's upper arm, her fingers gripping to prevent the DI from pulling away. "Beware, Yvonne Giles... You're going to meet him. There's danger."

"Well, yes... The killer is a very dangerous individual."

"There is danger for you." Penny leaned forward. Her breath smelled of coffee. "Don't see him on your own."

The DI pulled her arm free. Taking a gasp of air, after holding her breath, heart thumping in her chest. "I'll bear that in mind," she replied.

She moved away from Penny, feeling shaken despite suspecting the other woman of being unhinged. Her eyes wandered back to the numbered markers within the smaller cordon. She pushed her hands into her pockets of her coat, which she pulled more tightly about herself. In the trees, a crow cawed. She headed back to Dewi.

21

THE GIRLS IN THE MUD

Two hours later, SOCO and Hanson were on their knees in the dirt, sifting and photographing as they excavated two new graves. "I've asked for light and a generator," he explained to Yvonne. "We'll be at this long after it gets dark."

She nodded. "What have we got? Are they female?"

He ran the back of a forearm across his forehead. "It's a little too early to say for sure, but at first glance, looking at the pelvises, I'd say the likelihood is that these are young females who hadn't yet given birth. We'll get everything cleaned up, and see what we've got. If it's the same killer, and he used a blade again, we should see some evidence of that on the bones. The graves are several years old at least. All flesh is gone."

"I'll let you get on." Yvonne considered Psychic's words. Two females. Had she really seen them in a dream? Or did her knowledge come from elsewhere? She turned back to the pathologist. "I'll catch up with you tomorrow. The sooner I know more about those women, the better. How soon can we compare dental records?"

"We'll do the comparison early tomorrow." He cocked his head. "Do you have an idea who they might be?"

"I have a hunch." She nodded. "I'll be in touch tomorrow."

∼

THE DI TOSSED AND TURNED, soaking her bed sheets. Tasha was back in London and, at three o'clock in the morning, Yvonne was reluctant to wake her partner with a call or a text. Instead, she lay awake watching shadows on the ceiling, trying to forget her nightmare about Penny Farthing, graves, and a masked killer caked in blood.

At four o'clock, after sleep continued refusing to come, she gave up and made herself a cuppa.

The mug of tea and the lights flooding her kitchen lifted her spirits.

She thought about Simon Jones, wondering why he had attended the search that day.

She paid him a visit first thing.

∼

HE SAW her enter the store and disappeared amid the aisles. It made her more determined to speak to him.

Garvey-and-Griffiths was quiet, making it easy to give her the runaround. But, determined to ask him why he had attended the search, she didn't let that stop her.

Luckily for Yvonne, his height made it impossible to hide for long. She spotted his head above the shelving to her right. "Simon?"

He hesitated, as though going through his options.

"I won't keep you long. I only want a quick word."

He looked left, then right. "I'll come to you."

He joined her, shoulders hunched, and making only brief eye contact.

"We can go to the office," she suggested. "Out of the way."

"I don't know if-" Simon shot a look at the office door.

"I won't keep you long." She didn't wait for his reply.

Don Akeman brushed crumbs from his mouth before scrunching a packet and tossing it into the wastepaper bin beside his chair. "Hello, Inspector." The colour rose in his cheeks. He shot a look at Simon.

"I wanted a quick word with Simon. Do you mind?" She cocked her head.

"Er... No, of course not." He picked up a pen from the desk and rose from his seat. "I'll go check on Dave on the shop floor." He narrowed his eyes at his colleague.

Yvonne cleared her throat.

"Right... I'll see you later." Don's stocky frame disappeared through the door.

"Do you know why I'm here, Simon?"

He shook his head, appearing childlike as he looked at his shoes, hands by his sides.

"I know you saw me on the field. You spotted me, then you left. I came to ask why?"

He grunted something inaudible.

"I don't understand this reaction, Simon. I know Mal was your colleague and your friend. You were bound to be curious. What I don't get is why you left when you saw us? Is something bothering you? Something you need to talk about?"

"I left Dave on his own."

"Sorry?"

He looked up. "Dave... He's part-time, and hasn't worked

here that long. I left him on his own, and I wasn't supposed to. Don wouldn't be happy if he knew. You won't tell him, will you?"

She rubbed her chin. "That depends on you, and whether you have told me everything you know."

His gaze returned to his feet.

"What made you go up to the fields? Knowing you would risk trouble at work? You could have left it until after you finished for the day?"

He shrugged.

"Were you curious about what we found?"

He didn't answer.

"Were you worried about what we might have found?"

No reply.

"Have you been there before, Simon?"

"No."

"Then why yesterday?"

"I was curious." He held his hands wide. "I wasn't the only one... Everybody wanted to know what was going on."

She pursed her lips. "Not everybody had to leave work to be there... Was there a particular reason for your curiosity?"

"No."

"Look..." The DI sighed. "I know you were here working the day Mal disappeared. There were many witnesses, and your alibi was as strong as they get. But did you know where Mal was heading when he left?"

"No."

"You see... I don't believe he went for a walk at all."

His eyes shot to hers.

"I think he nipped out to see a project, or to meet someone."

"Why do you think that?"

"Call it a hunch..."

"I wouldn't know."

"Really? See, I was wondering... If Mal popped out to see a client, my guess is he would have told you. You were the only other staff member here that day. He would have said something to you... Asked you to cover for him, like you asked Dave to cover for you, yesterday... You see where I'm coming from?"

He shrugged. "I don't remember."

"Your colleague and friend vanished, and that day didn't stick in your head? You'll forgive me for finding that hard to believe. Did he tell you where he was going? It's really important. We don't know whether he was killed in a random attack up the lane, or if he was killed somewhere else by a person he had agreed to meet that day." Her voice softened. "If we knew where he was killed, me could still recover DNA or other evidence. If you have knowledge of where he went, please tell us."

Jones opened his mouth, but closed it again.

"Have a think about it, Simon. If you know something more, you would let Mal down by not telling us. And, besides failing to disclose something important, you could be considered an accessory to murder. Here is my card." She handed it to him. "Call me."

∽

∽

Yvonne was sure Simon Jones was hiding something, and said so to Dewi when she got back.

"Like what?" he asked.

"I think he is protecting someone, or he's afraid of them.

I think he knows where Mal went that day. He's just not saying."

Her mobile vibrated on her desk. "Hi, Roger... What have you got?"

"The identity of both women?"

She sat upright in her chair. "You have? Fantastic work... Would their names be Nina Richards and Mair Harris?"

"What... How did you know? Did someone from my office leak it to you?"

"No, they didn't. The idea has been swirling around in the back of my mind for days. It wouldn't let me sleep last night. Both women went missing after Mal Edwards was murdered. I don't know how it all fits together yet, but I am increasingly sure that Mal not only knew his killer, but knew something incriminating about him. Mal's killer may have been building a shelter to keep women in that he had kidnapped. I think the bunker is somewhere underground, and Mal was killed because he guessed what the construction was for."

"Sounds plausible," Hanson agreed. "Do you want to come over? I can give you more details that may prove helpful. It'll be another day or two before I can send you my report."

"I'll be right over." She pocketed her phone and grabbed her jacket. "Dewi, can you hold the fort for me? I'm off to see Hanson. He says the remains are those of Nina Richards and Mair Harris."

"Oh, my God... Kate." Dewi put a hand to his forehead.

The DI nodded. "We've got to find her, and fast."

22

COMMON DENOMINATORS

The cleaned bones of Nina and Mair lay on separate steel trolleys in the mortuary.

Yvonne waited while Hanson replaced his gloves.

Free of mud, it was possible to tell that one girl had been in the soil for far longer than the other, judging by the staining of the bones.

"This one is Mair Harris, confirmed by her dental records." He adjusted his face mask, walking over to the other trolley. "And this is Nina Richards, again confirmed via dental records. We think they were put in the ground at separate times, with at least five years in between."

"Would you say they died at the time they went missing?" She joined him near the second trolley.

"Hard to say for sure. Dating is only accurate to within a few years, but I think neither of them had been in the ground for the whole of the time they were missing. We are working on a more accurate timeframe."

"How did they die?" Her eyes ran the length of the skeletons, some of the smaller bones were broken.

"They were each stabbed several times. I can't comment on any other injuries they might have sustained because of the absence of soft tissue. The weapon used may have been a hunting knife, not dissimilar to the one used to dispatch Malcolm Edwards."

"Could it have been the same weapon?"

"We're examining nicks in the bones under the electron microscope, and running spectroscopy on fragments. That is our best chance of confirming whether it is the same metal composition. But, in terms of size and shape? It could very well be the same knife."

"When will we know if it is identical?"

"I hope to confirm it later tomorrow."

"And the clothing? Do we have trace evidence?"

"SOCO has the garments. Both girls were fully clothed. There may be recoverable hair and fibres. Let's hope the killer still has some of his old clothing stashed in his wardrobe."

She pursed her lips. "Stabbing is up close and personal, and so is carrying and burying bodies. I've got everything crossed that there will have been a transfer."

"Do you have a suspect in mind?" Hanson pulled off his face mask.

"We have several suspects, but no-one who is directly in the frame. Any fibres or DNA you find, along with the composition of the metal in the blade, will be crucial." Her eyes went back to the bones. "I think these girls were held for some time, possibly years, before they were killed. I think we'll find that the same blade killed all three of our victims. Mal found out what was going on and paid for it with his life. If we find out who he confronted? We'll have our killer. In the meantime, I will speak to Mal's widow and find out if he and these women knew each other. As far as we know, Nina and Mair were abducted from the street. We don't know if they were stalked beforehand. If Mal knew the girls, and all three knew the killer, we might find a common denominator that leads us to the killer."

Hanson nodded. "I'll get on to the lab and remind them we need the results as soon as possible. I'll let you know the minute anything comes through."

"Thank you, Roger." Yvonne took one last look at the remains of what had been two bright young women with their whole lives ahead of them, before her thoughts turned to Kate Hughes and Kelly Lewis. They might still be incarcerated somewhere in an underground hellhole.

~

~

RHIANNON EDWARDS' curtains were open, but barely.

Yvonne eyed the trampled grass, kicked over flower pots and footprints in the flower bed. All were telltale signs of reporters chasing a story. Her heart went out to Mal's widow. The last few weeks had not been easy.

Dewi knocked on the door.

The curtain twitched.

Mrs Edwards opened the door, fiddling with her hastily fixed ponytail, several strands of which roamed freely. Her puffy eyes blinked in the sunlight.

She held her hand to her forehead. "Thank God you are the police. I thought I'd have to shout at more journalists. This place has gone crazy over the last few days."

"I know." Yvonne sighed. "I'm sorry, that's all you need. May we come in?"

Rhiannon stepped back. "I had a dreadful night. You'll

have to forgive the mess."

The DI eyed the leftovers of a takeaway which littered the coffee table in the lounge.

"Last night's tea…" Rhiannon pulled a face. "My son and daughter came over for moral support."

"I'm glad you've had company." Yvonne nodded. "Don't worry about the state of the house, Rhiannon. We're here to ask you some questions about Mal. We won't keep you long."

"Please, sit down." Mal's widow adjusted the cushions on the sofa, and moved the littered coffee table away, before sitting in an armchair opposite.

Yvonne took out her notebook. "You have most likely already heard, but we found more remains in the field where your husband was buried."

"I know." She took a shuddering breath. "It's why the reporters were back."

"We believe it to be two young women."

"Okay…"

"Do the names Nina Richards and Mair Harris mean anything to you?"

Mrs Edwards' forehead creased in thought. "They ring a bell… I don't know why. I didn't know them. Wait, didn't one of them go missing a while ago?"

"Yes, they both disappeared in the years after Mal vanished."

"I see."

"Can you tell us whether your husband knew either of those women?"

"I don't know… I would have said no, but I sometimes wonder whether I really knew him at all."

"The reason we ask is we believe the same person was responsible for all three murders, starting with your husband's. The killer may have been known to all three of victims."

"I know nothing about these girls. I don't know if Mal knew them. Unless he met them through work? Do you think he did? He wasn't seeing them, was he?" Rhiannon frowned.

Yvonne shook her head. "No, we are not saying that. We think there may have been a mutual connection. Mal might have confronted someone who was abducting or intending to abduct women. We think this because one of his former colleagues told us he was agitated following a visit to a client's project. We cannot go into detail at this stage, but we believe the project may have roused Mal's suspicions. Did he mention to you any concerns he may have had about a customer before he disappeared?"

Rhiannon gazed at the window. "I don't recall a conversation like that... I went over and over everything in my mind after he went, analysing all we'd said and done. I think I would have remembered if he had mentioned anything sinister. He must have kept it to himself."

"Perhaps he wasn't sure of his suspicions."

Mrs Edwards brought her eyes back to the officers. "If there was something bothering him, he would have wanted to protect me from it."

As they left Rhiannon's home, Yvonne couldn't help feeling they were missing something right under their noses.

Dai grabbed her as soon as they got back to the station. "Ma'am, Andrew Riley rang. After further analysis, they've found another anomaly in the geophysics data. Riley thinks there's another grave up there."

"Oh, no..." Her heart sank. "God, I hope it isn't Kelly or Kate."

"He says the data is not as clear cut as the previous anomalies, but he thinks SOCO should take a look."

She nodded. "I agree. I'll run it past the DCI, but it would be negligent not to investigate given what we have found up there already. Tell him to get on with it. I'll square it with the DCI."

Callum plopped copies of x-rays on her desk. "Hanson sent these over with his report. He said he's there all day if you need to speak with him in person."

"Thanks, Callum." She picked up the paperwork. "Have you had a look? What is he saying?"

"He has identified the type of knife we are looking for." The DC pointed to the x-rays. "He believes the same knife was used for all the victims. It is a single-edged blade, and he has narrowed it down to the type of knife sold for bush crafting. Particles of carbon-steel were still present in the nicks on the bones. It was consistent across all the remains... Same composition."

"So if we find the knife, we find the killer."

"Right."

"Bushcraft knife..." She frowned. "I'm not sure any of our suspects are known for bush crafting. Dig into it, Callum. Find out if anyone linked to these cases has reason to have such a knife."

"Will do."

She was impressed with the work the pathologist had put in. The painstaking measurements and reconstruction of the angles the blade was at as the injuries were inflicted. Particles left behind in the bones suggested the blade had been sharpened before each murder. The killer had left nothing to chance, using a weapon that was large enough to be lethal, but small enough to conceal until the last moment. The victims were unlikely to have seen it coming.

23

HELL

Kate could hear Kelly crying in the darkness. "Do you want to talk?" She asked, rubbing at her shackled wrist with her free one. "I'm still awake."

Kelly cleared her throat. "I'm sorry, Kate. I didn't mean to keep you from sleeping."

"You haven't," Kate reassured. "I couldn't sleep, anyway. I'm still thinking of how we'll get out of here."

The other woman smothered a sob.

"Please don't cry, Kelly. It's going to be all right, you'll see."

"Oh, Kate... I keep thinking that there's only one way out of here." She sobbed again. "And maybe when it comes, it will be a blessing. I can't take any more of this."

"Listen..." Kate propped herself up, bringing her mouth closer to the boards above her. "Don't give up, you hear me? We're going to think of a way out."

"You think?" Kelly quietened. "How?"

"Well, he's got to take the chain off you to take you out of here, correct?"

"I guess..."

"That will be our chance... I don't know what we're going to do. I still mull that over, but we will come up with a plan. We are not giving up without a fight, you hear me?"

"I hear you," Kelly answered.

Kate thought she detected a slight lift in her friend's voice. A sign of renewed hope. A hope, she was determined, would not become a disappointment.

∼

Mal waited at the bottom of the lane, checking his watch for the third time.

He had not expected the man to be late. A delayed start would mean getting back to the shop floor late, and he wasn't the sort to let anyone down. He'd been juggling a lot of balls lately. Something had to give, but what he had to say was too important to cancel this meeting now.

"Sorry I'm late."

The wide grin didn't look right. There was tension in that face. Mal hesitated.

"Have you changed your mind?" The other man frowned. "I would have got here sooner, only I had a puncture this morning. Had to be towed. I only just got the vehicle back. It's a heap of junk. I should have sold it at auction last month."

Mal took another look at his watch. "There's enough time, if we're quick."

The other man's shoulders relaxed. "I want your opinion on the ground, and to look at your ideas for the final plans. I've got most of the materials, but I'll need to ring you tomorrow with the rest of the list." He revved the engine. "I know what I want in my head, but I need your help to make it workable."

Mal climbed into the passenger seat. "Fine."

24

ANOTHER GRAVE?

Andrew Riley stood in a corner of the field, wearing a wax jacket and wellingtons, holding an iPad, and directing SOCO officers to the new area of interest.

Yvonne waved to him as he turned towards the marquee.

"The excavation is about to start," he advised. "We think there's something there, but the land falls away to the brook, so there's a chance it's not a body. The anomaly is not as big as the previous graves. But as I say, the land is uneven there and it could be skewing the results."

She grimaced. "And we couldn't get the cadaver dogs. They're busy elsewhere. But you think this is another grave, right?"

"I think it is. I've enough experience to say I'm fairly sure something or someone is buried there."

The DI scanned the landscape, her eyes following the hedgerows to the trees. "What about the rest of the field? Is it clear?"

He nodded. "I can say with a fair degree of certainty

there is nothing else here. All the graves are in that bottom section of the field, within ten metres of the gate, which makes sense." He scratched his head. "The field drops and levels off there. It's the part most hidden from view. Any further up, and he would have been visible from the road. He didn't need to worry about the farm, only passing vehicles. He most likely buried them at night."

"Okay, I'll let you get on." She nodded. "I'll check in with you later."

∼

"What have you got for me, Callum?" She threw her coat over the back of her chair.

"Wyn Thomas, the dairy farmer, has a sideline selling logs to locals."

"Okay…"

"He owns the woods at the top of his land, and received grants for planting a certain number of trees. He reduced the size of his pastureland, turning more of it into woodland, to get more government money."

"Why is that important? Ah… okay, the bush crafting knife?"

"Right." Callum put his hands in his pockets, shrugging his shoulders. "It's just an idea. Whoever owns the murder weapon, likely works or camps in woodland. None of our suspects go camping, but working in woodland could be a worthwhile angle to explore."

"Good work, Callum. I think we should pay Thomas a visit, ask him about his woodland, and find out what tools he uses. Can you ask Hanson for a photograph of the sort of knife we are looking for?"

"Do you want me to come with you?"

"Yes, please, we'll get up there as soon as Hanson sends the image. We can check on the Garthowen excavation on the way back. I am praying it's not Kate Hughes in that field."

Callum sighed. "You and me both."

25

MUDDIED WATERS

Wyn Thomas's nostrils flared. "Haven't I answered all of your questions? Do you really want to do this again?" He placed his hands on his hips, blocking the doorway. "This farm doesn't run itself."

"We appreciate that, Mister Thomas." Callum took a step forward. "We would still like a word, if we can?"

The farmer ran a hand through his hair. "Let's go into the yard. I don't want my wife worrying. She got upset after you came here last time." He led them out into the cobbled yard, surrounded on three sides by the farmhouse and outbuildings. "What can I help you with this time?"

Yvonne cleared her throat. "We understand you sell logs from the wood at the top of your land?"

"We own the woods up there, yes... It's perfectly legal." He scowled. "I'm not doing anything I shouldn't."

"Where do you keep your tools?" She kept her gaze on him.

"Tools? Which tools? The ones we use for logging?"

"The tools you use for forestry, yes."

He frowned. "I keep them in the big shed."

"Who has access to that shed?"

"Me, and a couple of young lads that work for me on and off."

"Anyone else?"

"No... What is this?"

"May we see inside your shed?"

"If you want to? It's just a shed, but if that will make you happy, I'll go get the keys."

He strode back to the house.

The DI pursed her lips. "He's not happy to have us poking around."

Callum nodded. "He's hiding something, or he's fed up with seeing us."

"Hang on, he's on his way back." She pushed her hand into her pocket. "Keep your eyes peeled for a four-inch blade."

"Will do."

Thomas held the keys up, swinging them back and forth to underline his frustration. "If I give you these, do you promise to leave me alone for a while?"

Callum took them from him.

Yvonne shook her head. "I can't promise you that. We are in the middle of a murder investigation, and those who knew the victims will be interviewed, and their dealings explored. However, if we find nothing, you can be ruled out of the investigation. We are grateful for your patience, Wyn. I know you haven't found this easy, but you said you liked Mal. Think of this as the last thing you can do for him. We all want his murderer brought to justice, don't we?"

"Of course."

"Then let's get this done." She nodded to Callum.

He took off the padlock.

The heavy door creaked and shuddered along its sliders. "This could do with some oil, Wyn," he suggested.

"Aye, I'll get the lads on it tomorrow."

Inside, the walls were lined with many types of equipment.

The DI took in the chainsaws, strimmers, saws, bow saws, scythes, shovels, rakes, and axes of various sizes.

In the middle of the room stood a large leaf shredder, a concrete mixer, ladders lying on their side, a pressure washer, and a large hose attached to one of the supporting beams.

"Do you have smaller tools in here, Wyn?" Callum asked, walking the length of the barn, examining items as he went.

Yvonne kept her eyes on Thomas.

"What sort of tools?" The farmer's eyes narrowed.

"Pruning saws? Shears? Knives?" Callum asked.

"They are on the wall at the back."

The DC walked to the end of the barn. "Are these all you have?"

"Yes, every tool we use for maintaining the woodland is in here."

"What about smaller knives? Do you have any of those?"

"You mean one of these?" Wyn lifted his jumper, revealing a sheathed knife on his belt.

"Yes." She eyed the knife. "Can we borrow that?"

"Will I get it back?" He undid his leather belt, removing the sheath.

"We'll get it back to you within a few days."

He sighed. "Well, make sure you do."

∼

"This one is different," Riley said, as Yvonne donned a plastic suit and overshoes.

"In what way?" She turned to where SOCO was busy excavating the new grave.

"It's a smaller hole..."

She frowned. "Oh, no... It's not a child, is it?"

He shook his head. "I don't know, you'd better ask them. I'm packing up here."

A pair of SOCO officers took samples of the soil. The DI headed over to them. "What have we got?" She cast her eyes over the tagged bags of discoloured bones and jars containing the samples.

One SOCO stood, brushing mud from his knees. "The remains have been moved previously."

"Moved?"

"We think so... The soil inside the skull is a different consistency. It's a darker, sandy loam. It's not the clay soil of these fields. We'll have to run the relevant tests, of course, but I believe the bones were moved here from another location."

"Do you have any idea when they were moved? Can you tell us where they were before?"

He shook his head. "The where can only be confirmed if we have soil samples to match it with. The when? From experience, I'd estimate some time in the last twelve to eighteen months. We've taken samples from around the grave, but I believe these remains were already reduced to bone before they were moved."

Yvonne nodded. "Well, that would explain why the grave was so small. I can see they belonged to an adult."

"An adult female, I would say. Young... Hanson can confirm that for you later. We'll get all this stuff back to the lab and run tests on the soil samples ASAP. Looks like your perp was spooked by something. They felt they had to move the remains."

"None of the other bodies were moved. I wonder why this one was?"

"Like I say, we'll confirm the details with you once we've had a proper look. Let you know as soon as we can."

"Thank you, I appreciate it." She looked over the undulating landscape, and down over the quiet estate below. Beyond it, she could hear teenagers yelping as they played on the high school playground at the opposite side of the estate. Most of their victims had been barely older than those kids. She prayed that fate would not be so cruel to those she could hear enjoying themselves down there.

One thing she was grateful for, she mused on the way back to the car. The remains could not be those of Kate Hughes. They had been buried too long ago. She felt sure that Kate was being held somewhere, just as she was sure the other victims had been. They had to find her before she suffered the same fate. The killer had moved those remains because he was afraid they would be discovered. They must have been on his home turf.

As she pushed her collar up against the wind, she wondered if the remains were those of Kelly Lewis. It would be days before she would discover the truth.

26

THE DEATH OF MAL

Mal got out of the truck, one eye on his companion, forming and reforming the right words in his mind. He would phrase it softly, in case he was wrong. No, soft wouldn't be right.

"Something up, Mal? You don't seem yourself." The man clunked his door shut, locking the vehicle.

"Where were you thinking of putting the shelter? You decided on the ultimate spot, yet?" Mal licked sweat from his upper lip.

"Come with me."

They had parked the truck in the driveway at the front of the property.

The customer led him around the side of the red-brick dwelling, to a sizeable back garden, surrounded by high hedging, mostly copper beech. It wasn't overlooked.

Mal swivelled round, heart pounding in his chest. The blood along his spine ran cold. "You've moved the shed…"

"I thought I'd use the spot underneath. The soil is deeper there," the other replied.

"Where is she?" Sweat pooled between Mal's shoulder blades.

"Where is who?" He asked, but there was no confusion lining his forehead, no distortion of his features.

"Diane."

"Diane?" Again, the man's demeanour was cool. Too cool.

"Diane Webb... You took her, didn't you? Is she in there?" Mal pointed to the house. "In the basement? In the attic?"

"What are you talking about, Mal? Have you lost your mind?" He took a step closer.

"I saw you..." Mal licked his upper lip, taking a step back. "I was coming out of the junction opposite the garage at Garthmyl, and I waved to you, but you didn't see me."

The other man glared at him. "So?"

"I knew what the time was. My daughter needed a lift, so I had to get home. I was running late."

"You're not making any sense." He took another step forward, his face giving nothing away.

"I saw her with blonde hair... in your passenger seat, and I didn't know who she was. I thought you'd found a new girlfriend until..."

"Until?"

"Until I saw the news... They said she'd left her boyfriend in the car, and gone to the customer toilet at the garage. He went into the shop, and when he came out... She wasn't there. But you were there, weren't you? I saw her head leaning against the window. What did you do to her? Where is she? Have you been taking photographs again?"

"Look, I don't know what you're talking about. Your imagination is running wild-"

"Then, there's this..." Mal pulled out his notebook. "You drew the original... The rough plan for your shelter. I copied it into my notebook. I realised later that this was no shelter."

"Of course it's a shelter. I-"

"With the opening mechanism on the outside? Really? How would you get out? How would anyone inside get out?"

"Now listen here-"

"I thought you joked when you said it could be an underground prison..."

"I did."

"I saw her. I saw the missing woman. She-"

Mal didn't see it coming. The blade tore into his gut. He looked down in disbelief, hands going to the knife as it pulled out and plunged in again, this time angled upwards.

He fell to his knees, eyes wide in horror.

"You should have kept your nose out of it. You should have picked up your daughter on time." The killer grabbed the back of Mal's head and pushed the dying man to the floor.

∼

∼

"Wyn's knife is not a match." Callum placed the forensic report on her desk. "It's not the one used on our victims. If Thomas killed those women, he must have used another weapon."

Yvonne flicked through the pages. Spectroscopy had confirmed the blade was not the same composition. She nodded. "I'm not surprised, Callum. Whoever abducted and killed those women has a garden. Nowhere on Thomas's farm would we find a composted, sandy loam. I think we can all but rule out our farmer."

"What would you like us to do now?" Callum pulled his hands out of his pockets.

"Get yourself to Bryn Ellis's old address on Milford

Road. Ask the family living there if they noticed any ground disturbance over the last twelve to eighteen months."

"What will you do?"

"Dewi and I will do the same at David Cadman's old address on Canal Road. Call me if your people have experienced anything like that. Ring me straight away."

"Will do."

27

THE MISSING CHRYSANTHEMUMS

Dewi drove them in the black BMW, staying just inside of the legal speed limit.

Yvonne had previously telephoned the Williams couple, now in their eighties, who occupied Cadman's former address.

They made the DI feel tall, both being under five-foot-five. They greeted the officers at the door, opening it before she and Dewi had even traversed the garden path.

Yvonne couldn't help smiling, despite the urgency of their visit.

They sat in a well-proportioned lounge, sunlight streaming in from a large window.

"You told me on the phone you had plants stolen twelve months ago?" She pulled out her notebook.

"Yes." Clive Williams nodded. "I didn't think we'd hear any more of it, to be honest with you. A very nice police officer came to see us when it happened, but he had little hope of us getting our chrysanthemums back. We had two small acer trees in there, too. Beautiful purple leaves, they had. The thieves took them as well... Dug the lot up. I'm impressed you're all still on the case, like." He beamed at them.

Yvonne swallowed. "Er... We're not here with the answers to who took your plants, I'm afraid. However, we may very well solve your case when we solve our own. Ours is a murder mystery."

Owen Williams stared at the DI, open-mouthed. "Are you saying our plant thief has killed someone? Why would stealing our chrysanthemums lead to murder?"

The DI held back a smile. "It's more complicated than that, I feel." She leaned forward on the sofa. "We have reason to suspect that human remains were buried in your garden... They're not there now." She held up a hand at their shocked faces. "But they may have been. Your lost plants might have been the consequence of those remains being dug up and removed. It's likely they were removed from your ground so they wouldn't be discovered."

"Oh Lord, we didn't know..." Clive sat back in his chair, wide-eyed. "We had only just planted the chrysanthemums..."

Yvonne nodded. "It is possible that our killer was spooked by your digging and planting of the ground. I am sorry to give you this news. We will have to dig your patch up again, I'm afraid, as we will need to take soil samples. There may be police dogs, too. If human remains were buried here, it would have been several years ago, perhaps even decades ago. I must ask you to keep all of this under your hat until we have brought our perpetrator to justice."

"We will. No problem, Inspector." Clive nodded.

"There will be police personnel visiting your garden, including SOCO officers, dressed in plastic suits. Please don't be alarmed by that. It is nothing for you to worry about. We will keep you informed every step of the way."

"What if he comes back?" Olwen asked.

"If we find anything here, we'll be taking the perpetrator into custody."

"You know who he is, then?"

"We have our suspicions, yes. We need important evidence from for your garden in order to be sure."

"Right..." Clive rubbed his neck. "Mum's the word until you've got him in the bag."

"Thank you." She smiled. "In the meantime, we'll be monitoring you. You'll be perfectly safe."

∽

Yvonne paced the station floor in stockinged feet, having slipped off her shoes to cool them down.

Dewi sat at his desk, downing another coffee, and tapping his pen on the paperwork in front of him. He looked at his watch for the tenth time and sighed. "I thought they would have had the results through by now... They know it could be the difference between us finding Kate Hughes alive, or dead."

"Patience, Dewi..." The DI squeezed his shoulder. "They know we're waiting. I'm confident we'll get the results as soon as they do. They've never let us down before. They're staying late for our benefit, so let's give them a little while longer."

"Fine." He leaned back in his chair, hands behind his head. "It's just so hard sitting here when we know that young woman's life is on the line."

"I know. At least Llewelyn has organised the warrant. The judge will sign it as soon as we have confirmation that Cadman buried those remains. Sit tight... It will come. Besides, we haven't heard from our backup team yet."

"Email's in!" Dewi lunged for the mouse, opening the report.

"Soil samples?"

"Not yet. They've compared the latest remains with Kelly Lewis's dental records... It's not her."

"It's not?" Yvonne peered over his shoulder. "Then who is it?"

"Person unknown... They haven't found a match yet. They're going through the national databases. They said in the meantime, they are sending us the soil results."

The DI checked her watch. It was two minutes past nine at night. "I'll let the DCI know we're nearly ready-"

"I'm here." Chris Llewelyn stood in the doorway. "I came to see what was happening."

"They're sending through the soil results any minute."

"Great." He nodded. "I've got the Judge Jarman on standby."

"Got them," Dewi announced. "It's been confirmed... The soil samples from the Williams' garden match, and they found a human metatarsal bone which they are running DNA tests on. We don't have to wait for those, do we?"

Yvonne looked at the DCI. "I think we have enough, sir."

"I agree, and I don't think we should wait any longer. I'll get the warrant sent through, and we'll get over to Llanfyllin. Yvonne, can you make sure the armed units are ready to meet us in fifteen?"

"Will do, sir."

Twenty minutes later, they were pouring into the vans that would transport them to David Cadman's home.

"We'll cover all buildings at the same time." Llewelyn scanned their plan of action. "So, that's the house - front and back, the cube workshop, and the shed. As soon as Cadman is located and secured, we can concentrate on finding the girls."

Yvonne nodded, her throat dry. She eyed the armed officer opposite. "Be careful going in, won't you? The girls will be terrified."

She received only a nod, but that was enough. Armed response were focussed on the task, mentally preparing themselves for whatever lay ahead. His nod was more than enough.

28

LIFE OR DEATH?

They heard scraping above. He was coming back.

"Oh, no..." Kelly swallowed hard, her free hand reaching down for Kate's. "I think he's coming for me."

The two women shivered. They had known this time was coming. Friday had arrived.

"I was hoping he'd changed his mind." Kelly whispered.

They had clenched their fists for hours that day, prepared for a fight. Nervous energy had taken its toll, and both were feeling exhausted.

"Maybe he won't come down here," Kate cocked her head, listening.

Her hope was shattered when they heard the creaking that always preceded his descent.

"No..." Kelly squeezed Kate's hand.

"We're not taking this lying down." Kate sat upright on her bunk, pulling on her chain to get as near as possible to the entrance. "We'll hit him with everything we've got. Remember, he has to release you from your chain. You'll have two hands free, and I have got one. He's only got two, remember that."

"I'll try my best, Kate." Kelly dried her face. It stung from the salt in her tears and the cold air.

"I'll pretend to be asleep," Kate added, as the hatch opened.

～

"It's a text from Roger." Yvonne showed Dewi her phone. "They have the results from the soil samples. They match the Williams' garden."

"That's good to know." Dewi grinned. "It would be a bit late now if they didn't."

She checked her watch and swallowed hard. "We should be there in under fifteen."

They were thrown forward as the van took a roundabout at speed, sirens blaring. A helmet rolled across the floor.

The DI found it disconcerting, sitting side-on in a speeding vehicle.

An armed officer opposite retrieved his helmet, brushing it down with a gloved hand before holding it in his lap, and peering through the grill at the road ahead.

They were close. The roads were narrow and winding. The sirens were silent, though the lights still flashed their warning. Stealth would now be paramount if they were to save the girls.

Yvonne put a hand to her chest, her heart racing. She took several discrete deep breaths, her eyes flicking to the officer opposite. A panic attack was the last thing any of them needed.

～

He entered the bunker feet-first, negotiating the rungs of the ladder via a head torch.

Kate watched him descend, holding her breath, watching for the right moment. If she went for him too soon, he would easily overcome her. Better to wait until he released Kelly. He wouldn't see it coming.

"Get up!" He slapped the top bunk, yanking at the chain securing Kelly to the wall.

She cried out as pain shot through her chaffed wrist.

"I'm going to unlock this." The words were delivered in a growl. "Any nonsense, and you'll have a lot more than a sore arm."

He turned the key, and the shackle fell.

"Now!" Kate yelled, grabbing hold of their captor with her free arm. "Hit him, Kelly." She did her best to pull his legs from under him.

Kelly grabbed his hair, hitting him in the face with the iron shackle that no longer encased her wrist.

The surrounding air thickened with the stench of sweat and stress.

He hit out in all directions, staying on his feet, and punching Kelly to the head. She fell backwards into the wall. He turned his attention to Kate, putting both hands around her neck and squeezing.

The younger woman fought for breath, eyes bulging as she struggled for air past the painful pressure he exerted.

"Wait... Stop..." Kelly cried. "I'll go with you. I'm coming down. Please stop hurting her." She swallowed another sob. "Please stop."

29

THE BUNKER

Five minutes out of Llanfyllin, the team checked their equipment and killed the blue lights.

Yvonne and Dewi's van was the second of three making their way to the property.

Armed response strapped on their helmets as the vans turned into his lane.

Parking one behind the other, the side doors opened.

DCI Llewelyn strode towards the DI and Dewi from the first van. Everyone else moved to surround the house.

Having only their stab vests for protection, the three from CID followed behind the armed men. David Cadman had murdered four people that they knew of. They were taking no chances.

They entered through the garden gate, taking up positions close to the hedge, observing the armed officers as they settled into place.

Four officers approached the front door holding an enforcer, a sixteen-kilogram hardened-steel battering ram. They tapped each other on the shoulder before swinging it at the door, smashing the lock. "Go, go, go!"

The door swung open.

"Armed police!" They filed into the house, assault rifles at the ready. "Armed police, come down with your hands up!"

The house was in darkness, save for the torches on the officers' helmets and guns.

Yvonne watched the flashlights go from window to window. Though she could see her breath on the night air, sweat pooled below her stab vest. "Where is he?" she whispered to Dewi, as two ambulances joined their vehicles in the lane.

"Either he's hiding, or he's not in."

"His truck is over there..." She pointed to the black Ford Ranger parked in the drive.

"I'll do a vehicle check, see if he has any others registered to him."

"Thanks." Her eyes moved back to the house, where officers began filing out.

Their leader approached the DCI. "He's not there."

"Okay." Llewelyn scratched his head, turning to Yvonne. "What are your thoughts?"

"We should search the other buildings, and every patch of ground. I am sure there is a bunker here. We have to find the opening."

Dewi interrupted them. "He's the registered owner of a silver Nissan." He told the registration. "It's not here, so he must be somewhere in the Nissan."

"Right..." Llewelyn placed his hands on his hips. "Put out an all-persons... Tell them to keep an eye out for the silver Nissan. In the meantime, we need all CCTV monitors watching the main roads. Yvonne?"

"Sir?"

"Do you know where he might have gone?"

She shook her head. "No... I really think we should search this property for the bunker right now."

"What if it isn't here?"

She shook her head. "It is. Why would he take the trouble to build it elsewhere when he can be here, and private?" He swept her arms around. "He's not overlooked. The garden is protected by high hedges, and we are at least three hundred yards from the nearest neighbour. If he has been keeping women in a bunker, he'll have done so somewhere where he can have complete control, away from prying eyes. I think that place is here, on his home turf."

"I see your point." Llewelyn had a word with the armed response inspector, before turning back to Yvonne and Dewi. "We'll search here. There's a dog team on the way. They can help. We'll have officers out on the road, in case he comes back."

"Great." She nodded. "We're looking for a basement, or a hatch in the ground. We should scour every inch."

It wasn't easy in the dark. The DI used her maglite torch in the garden, leaving the house to uniformed officers, and the cube to the DCI and Dewi.

She was drawn once more to the triangular end of the garden and the secluded area with the old shed. The grass had grown to half-way up her shin, but it had been flattened in a narrow line running up to the shed door. The entrance was padlocked.

Yvonne looked around for something with which to break the lock, but found nothing near her, aside from a three or four old garden canes.

She headed over to the cube to find Dewi and the DCI.

"Found anything?" Llewelyn asked.

"I need something to force open a padlock."

"Will this do?" Dewi grabbed a crowbar from a hook on

the wall. "Are you okay with using this? Or would you like some help?"

She pressed her lips together. "I think I'd be okay getting it open, but I would like your presence if possible?"

Dewi glanced at the DCI.

"Go ahead... I can carry on here."

It took several attempts to force the padlock, but they finally cracked open the ten-by-six feet shed. For such a battered-looking hut, the door hinges were remarkably smooth.

Dewi looked around the inside. "The shelves are full..."

"Yes, and the floor isn't. Don't you think that is odd? Do you know anyone whose shed is virtually empty? It bothered me when I first saw it. I made him lift the grass matting. I was so sure there'd be a trapdoor underneath."

"Well..." Dewi grabbed the folded workbench. "Let's get this bench and chairs out of here and lift the matting again. Perhaps you missed something? If there is an opening, it's bound to be well hidden."

Breath clouding around their heads, they carried out the two meagre pieces of furniture.

The grass matting lifted with ease. They dumped it on the ground outside, turning their attention to the wooden floor, scouring it with torchlight.

"There's nothing obvious... No hatch." She examined the edges, where the floorboards abutted the sides of the hut. "Wait..." She turned to Dewi. "Do you have that crowbar?"

He retrieved it from outside. "There you go."

"We need to exit. There's something I want to try."

Once outside, she wedged the end of the crowbar between the edge of the floor and the frame at the base of the wall, pushing it in as far as she could, before applying her weight to lever it up.

To both their surprise, the floor lifted with ease. After raising the end by a couple of inches, they could get their fingers underneath, hoisting and pushing it up, until they could lean it against the back wall.

Below their feet was now a concrete floor, at the centre of which was a round hatch with a push lock handle. The latch you find on a walk-in cold room. They exchanged glances.

"Let's get it open." Yvonne grabbed the handle, yanking until it gave.

They peered into the darkness below.

30

HUNTING A KILLER

The DI shone her torch inside. "Hello? Is anybody down there?"

"Yes." A cracked female voice emanated from below.

"I am Yvonne Giles. I am a police officer. We're coming down. Is anybody with you?"

"No."

Yvonne turned to Dewi. "Let the DCI know we've found the bunker and get the paramedics here."

"On it." Her sergeant disappeared.

She climbed down the ladder, torch clamped between her teeth, to join the woman below. "Are you injured?" She asked.

The woman's matted hair clung to her tear-stained face. Around her neck, thick red welts and bruising suggested she had suffered a recent trauma. She was shackled to the wall and covered by only a blanket.

"My name is Kate. Kate Hughes."

The DI put her arm around the trembling girl. "We're

getting you out of here, Kate. Medics are on their way. You're safe now."

"He's got Kelly... He's got her, you've got to stop him." More tears fell down her face.

"Kelly? Do you mean Kelly Lewis?"

"Yes, they left not that long ago. He's going to kill her. Please, find him." She pulled at her chain. "He's taken her somewhere."

"Okay, listen, Kate... I can hear the medics. I am going to climb out of here, so we can try to find your friend. The ambulance staff will get you out of here and take you to the hospital. They can contact your family. We will be along to see you as soon as we can but, in the meantime, we have to go find David Cadman before he harms Kelly. Do you know where he might have taken her?"

"No, I don't. They left about an hour ago, I think. I don't have any way to measure time down here. But he is going to kill her unless you stop him."

"We'll get right onto it." Yvonne gave Kate a hug before climbing the ladder to allow the paramedics down.

She crossed the garden to where Dewi was deep in conversation with the DCI. "He's got Kelly Lewis with him. Kate thinks he intends to kill her tonight. We have very little time."

"Right." Llewelyn called the armed response team over the radio, requesting officers to go with them to look for Cadman. "Is everybody ready to go?" he asked the DI and Dewi. "The minute that car is seen, we're going to chase it down."

"I'm good." Yvonne nodded.

"I'm requesting a helicopter." Llewelyn grabbed his mobile. "If they follow his car, he won't be able to harm the girl without them seeing him do it. He won't want to risk that."

~

"Where are we going?" Kelly's back throbbed from being bunched up in the passenger footwell. Her wrists and ankles burned from bonds too tight.

"Where no-one will find you." His harsh tone silenced her. She could see his hand on the gear stick, and the occasional street light whizzing past.

The car made a sharp right turn and slowed. He had driven on to a smaller, winding road and they were climbing. She counted seconds in her head, an attempt to measure how far they had travelled, all the while saying her goodbyes to those she loved as though they were with her.

He didn't speak, eyes remaining on the road.

~

"The Nissan's been spotted by CCTV on the Welshpool bypass, heading towards Newtown. A traffic car is close to his position, heading from Berriew and should be on him soon. More cars are on their way from Newtown." Dewi turned his radio up.

They piled into the vans, heading out towards Newtown. They were some twenty minutes behind.

Yvonne no longer noticed the jolting of the vehicle. A young woman's life hung in the balance. That was all that mattered.

"I can hear the chopper." Dewi strained to listen. "That probably means they've located-"

He was interrupted by radios bursting into life. "Nissan located, five miles out of Llanfair Caereinion, over."

"We're at least twenty minutes away from Llanfair," Yvonne said, looking at her watch.

DCI Llewelyn spoke with control regarding units in the area, then turned to her. "A mobile unit is in pursuit, with another heading through Llanfair to block him off from that direction. If they get to the junction ahead of him, they'll deploy the stingers," he said, referring to the chain of spikes used to burst the tyres of speeding vehicles, bringing them to a halt.

Yvonne nodded. "So long as Kelly isn't put at risk."

31

NOWHERE TO RUN

Erratic motion, and the fumes from the vehicle, had taken their toll on Kelly. She vomited in the footwell.

"Christ, you dirty-" He didn't finish. His attention was grabbed by a beam of light surrounding them. He could hear the helicopter overhead, and put his foot down hard on the accelerator.

Kelly's head hit the underside of the dashboard. She closed her eyes, lying still as she could to reduce the overwhelming nausea and pain in her stomach. The stench of vomit was unbearable.

His pace did not relent. She could feel the vibrations coming through the floor as he pushed the car to its limits. "Please, God," Kelly whispered. "I don't want to die."

A loud pop reverberated through the car, followed by a hissing. The car slewed sideways, coming to a halt on the verge.

Kelly kept her eyes closed, convinced they must have crashed. Perhaps she was so injured she couldn't feel anything.

The engine continued to purr.

The young woman opened her eyes as her captor opened his door, making a run for it.

Shouting hailed from several directions. Everything around her flashed blue in the lights from emergency vehicles.

Kelly laughed and cried, lifting her head up to be seen, relieved when she saw the first officer through the driver's window.

∽

When their van arrived, Yvonne, Dewi, and the DCI were greeted by the sight of Cadman bent over the bonnet of a police vehicle, being cuffed from behind.

"Where's Kelly?" The DI ran towards the arresting officer. "There was a woman with him. Where is she?"

The PC dragged Cadman from the vehicle by an arm, pointing to the ambulance further along the lane. "She's being checked over. I'd be quick. They're taking her to Shrewsbury hospital."

"Right." Yvonne ran to the back of the ambulance, where Kelly stood, wrapped in a blanket while they readied a wheelchair for her.

"Kelly? Kelly Lewis?"

The girl turned to the DI, her blonde hair tangled, eyes large. "Yes..."

"You don't know me. I'm Detective Inspector Yvonne Giles. I'm so glad to see you're okay."

"My friend Kate, is she-"

"She's safe... We found her. She told us Cadman had taken you, and that you were in danger."

"She was so brave…" Kelly's gaze dropped to the road.

"Your family will be ecstatic you're alive."

Kelly's eyes met the DI's. "Are they okay? Do they know yet?"

"If they haven't been told already, they soon will be. We'll make sure they know within the hour. For now, you need looking after in hospital. We can talk to you about everything later."

A male paramedic seated Kelly in the wheelchair, which he pushed into the ambulance.

Yvonne waved as the doors closed.

"That's one lucky girl…" Dewi was at the DI's shoulder.

"Lucky?" Yvonne narrowed her eyes.

"I just mean she came so close to… Well, you know. If we hadn't got to Kate when we did, we wouldn't have known he was about to kill her."

"I know what you mean, Dewi. She was unlucky running into Cadman seven years ago, but luckily we got to her in time. It could so easily have ended differently."

∼

THE NEXT TIME Yvonne saw Kelly and Kate, it was through the tiny windows in the double-door to their ward in Shrewsbury hospital.

A nurse in blue scrubs squeezed hand gel into her palms, rubbing them together. "Are you okay?" She asked. "Do you want to visit someone?"

The DI looked at the two recovering women, surrounded by their families, smiling and catching up.

"No…" She shook her head. "I wanted to ask questions, but it can wait."

"Right, if you're sure?" The nurse gave her a smile before walking through the doors and onto the ward.

Yvonne turned away, back to the corridor from which she'd entered.

~

DCI LLEWELYN FOUND her back in CID.

"That was a brilliant result last night, Yvonne. Well done to you and the team."

"Thank you, sir."

"You know they found Ahmed Syeed?"

"They did?" She picked up her coffee, hoping the heat and caffeine would help clear her bleary eyes.

"He was staying with a cousin in Wolverhampton."

"A real cousin?"

"I doubt it, probably a friend. But he and Reza Hassani have another appeal hearing for asylum."

"Very good…" She turned to gaze through the window.

"Are you okay?" Llewelyn cocked his head to see her eyes.

"I'm fine, sir. I've been thinking about the rest of Cadman's victims… Mal, Nina, Mair, and his first victim. The one he buried in his garden on Canal Road. She's been identified as Diane Webb. She disappeared from a garage forecourt while holidaying near Welshpool."

Llewelyn nodded. "Thank God he's in custody. He won't see the light of day again."

"Another killer off the streets." She should have felt elation, but sadness had dogged her on this case. Perhaps it was the number of lives senselessly taken. That, and the fact Tasha had not yet returned from London.

She gave herself a mental shake. Two women were alive and reunited with their families. That was a reason for celebration. Yvonne decided she would take Dewi, Callum, Dai, and the DCI for a much-needed drink.

∼

THE END

AFTERWORD

Mailing list: You can join my emailing list here : AnnamarieMorgan.com

Facebook page: AnnamarieMorganAuthor

You might also like to read the other books in the series:
Book 1: Death Master:

After months of mental and physical therapy, Yvonne Giles, an Oxford DI, is back at work and that's just how she likes it. So when she's asked to hunt the serial killer responsible for taking apart young women, the DI jumps at the chance but hides the fact she is suffering debilitating flashbacks. She is told to work with Tasha Phillips, an in-her-face, criminal psychologist. The DI is not enamoured with the idea. Tasha has a lot to prove. Yvonne has a lot to get over. A tentative link with a 20 year-old cold case brings them closer to the truth but events then take a horrifyingly personal turn.

Book 2: You Will Die

After apprehending an Oxford Serial Killer, and almost losing her life in the process, DI Yvonne Giles has left England for a quieter life in rural Wales. Her peace is shattered when she is asked to hunt a priest-killing psychopath, who taunts the police with messages inscribed on the corpses. Yvonne requests the help of Dr. Tasha Phillips, a psychologist and friend, to aid in the hunt. But the killer is one step ahead and the ultimatum, he sets them, could leave everyone devastated.

Book 3: Total Wipeout

A whole family is wiped out with a shotgun. At first glance, it's an open-and-shut case. The dad did it, then killed himself. The deaths follow at least two similar family wipeouts – attributed to the financial crash.

So why doesn't that sit right with Detective Inspector Yvonne Giles? And why has a rape occurred in the area, in the weeks preceding each family's demise? Her seniors do not believe there are questions to answer. DI Giles must therefore risk everything, in a high-stakes investigation of a mysterious masonic ring and players in high finance.

Can she find the answers, before the next innocent family is wiped out?

Book 4: Deep Cut

In a tiny hamlet in North Wales, a female recruit is murdered whilst on Christmas home leave. Detective Inspector Yvonne Giles is asked to cut short her own leave, to investigate. Why was the young soldier killed? And is her death related to several alleged suicides at her army base? DI Giles this it is, and that someone powerful has a dark secret they will do anything to hide.

Book 5: The Pusher

Young men are turning up dead on the banks of the River Severn. Some of them have been missing for days or even weeks. The only thing the police can be sure of, is that the men have drowned. Rumours abound that a mythical serial killer has turned his attention from the Manchester canal to the waterways of Mid-Wales. And now one of CID's own is missing. A brand new recruit with everything to live for. DI Giles must find him before it's too late.

Book 6: Gone

Children are going missing. They are not heard from again until sinister requests for cryptocurrency go viral. The public must pay or the children die. For lead detective Yvonne Giles, the case is complicated enough. And then the unthinkable happens...

Book 7: Bone Dancer

A serial killer is murdering women, threading their bones back together, and leaving them for police to find. Detective Inspector Yvonne Giles must find him before more innocent victims die. Problem is, the killer wants her and will do anything he can to get her. Unaware that she, herself, is is a target, DI Giles risks everything to catch him.

Book 8: Blood Lost

A young man comes home to find his whole family missing. Half-eaten breakfasts and blood spatter on the lounge wall are the only clues to what happened...

Book 9: Angel of Death

He is watching. Biding his time. Preparing himself for a

torturous kill. Soaring above; lord of all. His journey, direct through the lives of the unsuspecting.

The Angel of Death is nigh.

The peace of the Mid-Wales countryside is shattered, when a female eco-warrior is found crucified in a public wood. At first, it would appear a simple case of finding which of the woman's enemies had had her killed. But DI Yvonne Giles has no idea how bad things are going to get. As the body count rises, she will need all of her instincts, and the skills of those closest to her, to stop the murderous rampage of the Angel of Death.

Book 10: Death in the Air

Several fatal air collisions have occurred within a few months in rural Wales. According to the local Air Accidents Investigation Branch (AAIB) inspector, it's a coincidence. Clusters happen. Except, this cluster is different. DI Yvonne Giles suspects it when she hears some of the witness statements but, when an AAIB inspector is found dead under a bridge, she knows it.

Something is way off. Yvonne is determined to get to the bottom of the mystery, but exactly how far down the treacherous rabbit hole is she prepared to go?

Book 11: Death in the Mist

The morning after a viscous sea-mist covers the seaside town of Aberystwyth, a young student lies brutalised within one hundred yards of the castle ruins.

DI Yvonne Giles' reputation precedes her. Having successfully captured more serial killers than some detectives have caught colds, she is seconded to head the murder investigation team, and hunt down the young woman's killer.

What she doesn't know, is this is only the beginning...

Book 12: Death under Hypnosis

When the secretive and mysterious Sheila Winters approaches Yvonne Giles and tells her that she murdered someone thirty years before, she has the DI's immediate attention.

Things get even more strange when Sheila states:

She doesn't know who.

She doesn't know where.

She doesn't know why.

Book 13: Fatal Turn

A seasoned hiker goes missing from the Dolfor Moors after recording a social media video describing a narrow cave he intends to explore. A tragic accident? Nothing to see here, until a team of cavers disappear on a coastal potholing expedition, setting off a string of events that has DI Giles tearing her hair out. What, or who is the thread that ties this series of disappearances together?

A serial killer, thriller murder-mystery set in Wales.

Book 14: The Edinburgh Murders

A newly-retired detective from the Met is murdered in a murky alley in Edinburgh, a sinister calling card left with the body.

The dead man had been a close friend of psychologist Tasha Phillips, giving her her first gig with the Met decades before.

Tasha begs DI Yvonne Giles to aid the Scottish police in solving the case.

In unfamiliar territory, and with a ruthless killer haunting the streets, the DI plunges herself into one of the darkest, most terrifying cases of her career. Who exactly is The Poet?

Book 15: A Picture of Murder

Men are being thrown to their deaths in rural Wales.

At first glance, the murders appear unconnected until DI Giles uncovers potential links with a cold case from the turn of the Millennium.

Someone is eliminating the witnesses to a double murder.

DI Giles and her team must find the perpetrator before all the witnesses are dead.

Book 16: The Wilderness Murders

People are disappearing from remote locations.

Abandoned cars, neatly piled belongings, and bizarre last photographs, are the only clues for what happened to them.

Did they run away? Or, as DI Giles suspects, have they fallen prey to a serial killer who is taunting police with the heinous pieces of a puzzle they must solve if they are to stop the wilderness murderer.

Book 17: The Bunker Murders

A murder victim found in a shallow grave has DI Yvonne Giles and her team on the hunt for both the killer and a motive for the well-loved man's demise.

Yvonne cannot help feeling the killing is linked to a string of female disappearances stretching back nearly two decades.

Someone has all the answers, and the DI will stop at nothing to find them and get to the bottom of this perplexing mystery.

Remember to watch out for Book 18, coming soon...

Printed in Great Britain
by Amazon